THE
DISREPUTABLE
HISTORY
OF
Frankie Landau-Banks

THE
DISREPUTABLE
HISTORY
OF
Frankie Landau-Banks

a novel by

E. LOCKHART

HYPERION
NEW YORK

Designed by Elizabeth H. Clark

1 3 5 7 9 10 8 6 4 2
This book is set in Granjon.
Printed in the United States of America
Library of Congress Cataloging-in-Publication Data on file.
ISBN-13: 978-0-7868-3818-9
ISBN-10: 0-7868-3818-3

Visit www.hyperionteens.com

For my college friends Kate, Polly, Cliff,
Aaron, and Catherine, who know all about
golf course parties and midnight adventures

A PIECE OF EVIDENCE

◉

December 14, 2007

To: Headmaster Richmond and the Board of Directors,
    Alabaster Preparatory Academy

I, Frankie Landau-Banks, hereby confess that I was the
sole mastermind behind the mal-doings of the Loyal
Order of the Basset Hounds. I take full responsibility for
the disruptions caused by the Order—including the
Library Lady, the Doggies in the Window, the Night of a
Thousand Dogs, the Canned Beet Rebellion, and the
abduction of the Guppy.

That is, I wrote the directives telling everyone what
to do.

I, and I alone.

No matter what Porter Welsch told you in his statement.

Of course, the dogs of the Order are human beings with free will. They contributed their labor under no explicit compunction. I did not threaten them or coerce them in any way, and if they chose to follow my instructions, it was not because they feared retribution.

You have requested that I provide you with their names. I respectfully decline to do so. It's not for me to pugn or impugn their characters.

I would like to point out that many of the Order's escapades were intended as social criticism. And that many of the Order's members were probably diverted from more self-destructive behaviors by the activities prescribed them by me. So maybe my actions contributed to a larger good, despite the inconveniences you, no doubt, suffered.

I do understand the administration's disgruntlement over the incidents. I see that my behavior disrupted the smooth running of your patriarchal establishment. And yet I would like to suggest that you view each of the Loyal Order's projects with the gruntlement that should attend the creative civil disobedience of students who are politically aware and artistically expressive.

I am not asking that you indulge my behavior; merely that you do not dulge it without considering its context.

Yours sincerely,

Frances Rose Landau-Banks

Frances Rose Landau-Banks,
class of 2010

SWAN

◉

THOUGH NOT, IN HINDSIGHT, so startling as the misdeeds she would perpetrate when she returned to boarding school as a sophomore, what happened to Frankie Landau-Banks the summer after her freshman year was a shock. Certainly upsetting enough to disturb Frankie's conservative mother, Ruth, and to rile several boys in Frankie's New Jersey neighborhood to thoughts (and even actions) they'd never before contemplated.

Frankie herself was unsettled as well.

Between May and September, she gained four inches and twenty pounds, all in the right places. Went from being a scrawny, awkward child with hands too big for her arms, a frizz of unruly brown fluff on her head, and a jaw so sharp it made Grandma Evelyn cluck about how "When it comes to plastic surgery, it never hurts to do these things before college," to being a curvaceous young woman with an offbeat look that boys found distinctly appealing. She grew into her angular face, filled out her figure, and transformed from a homely child into a loaded potato—all while sitting quietly in a suburban hammock, reading the short stories of Dorothy Parker and drinking lemonade.

The only thing Frankie herself had done to facilitate the change was to invest in some leave-in conditioner to tame the frizz. She wasn't the kind of girl to attempt a makeover. She had been getting along okay at Alabaster Prep without one, despite the fact that their boarding school was (as her older sister Zada pointed out) an institution where the WASPs outnumbered the other Protestants ten to one, the Catholics were pretty much in the closet, and the members of "the tribe" had largely changed their names from things like Bernstein to things like Burns.

Frankie had gotten by at Alabaster on the strength of being Zada's little sister. Zada was a senior when Frankie started, and though she'd never been outlandishly popular, Zada had a solid crew of friends and a reputation for speaking her mind. She'd let Frankie tag along with her group of juniors and seniors for the first part of the school year, and made it clear to everyone that Frankie was not to be messed with. Zada had let her little sister sit with her at lunch on an as-needed basis, and introduced her to people from the crew team, the lacrosse team, student government, and the debate team. This last group Frankie joined—and proved to be a surprisingly sharp competitor.

Frankie had held up her part of the bargain freshman year by not embarrassing Zada any more than she could help. She wore the clothes Zada told her to, did fine in her classes, and made friends with a group of mildly geeky fellow freshmen who were neither ostentatiously silly nor tragically lame.

By summer's end, when she saw Zada off to Berkeley, Frankie was curvy, lithe, and possessed of enough oomph to stop teenage boys in the street when they passed her. But if we are to accurately chronicle Frankie's transformation and so-called misbehavior in these pages, it is important to note that her physical maturation was not, at first, accompanied by similar mental developments. Intellectually, Frankie was not at all the near-criminal mastermind who created the Fish Liberation Society, and who will, as an adult, probably go on to head the CIA, direct action movies, design rocket ships, or possibly (if she goes astray), preside over a unit of organized criminals. At the start of sophomore year, Frankie Landau-Banks was none of these things. She was a girl who liked to read, had only ever had one boyfriend, enjoyed the debate team, and still kept gerbils in a Habitrail. She was highly intelligent, but there was nothing unusually ambitious or odd about her mental functioning.

Her favorite food was guacamole and her favorite color was white.

She had never been in love.

A Chance Encounter
that Would Prove Seminal

◉

HE DAY AFTER Zada departed for Berkeley, Frankie and her mother went to the Jersey Shore for a four-day weekend with Frankie's two divorced uncles and three cousins. They rented a creaky five-bedroom house on a tiny plot of cement, two blocks from the beach and boardwalk.

Frankie's cousins were all between the ages of ten and thirteen. And they were all boys. A pack of vile creatures, in Frankie's view, given to pummeling one another, throwing food, farting, and messing with Frankie's stuff unless she locked the door of her bedroom.

Every day, the whole group lugged beach chairs, blankets, pretzels, cans of beer (for the uncles), juice boxes, and sports equipment down to the shore, where they parked themselves for a solid six hours. Frankie couldn't read a novel without having a sand crab placed on her knee, a bucket of saltwater dumped on her abdomen, or a box of grape juice spilled on her towel. She couldn't swim without some cousin trying to grab her legs or splashing her. She couldn't eat without one of the boys nipping a chip off her plate or kicking sand across her food.

On the last day of the vacation, Frankie lay on a beach blanket listening to her balding, gently paunchy uncles discuss the Jackals' minor-league season. Frankie's mother dozed in a beach chair. For the moment, at least, the cousins were in the water, having breath-holding contests and occasionally trying to drown one another.

"Can I go into town?" Frankie asked.

Ruth lifted her sunglasses off her face and squinted at her daughter. "How come?"

"To walk around. Get an ice cream. Maybe buy some postcards," Frankie answered. She wanted to get away from all of them. The togetherness, the sports talk, the farting and pummeling.

Ruth turned to one of her brothers. "Ben, isn't it, like, fifteen blocks to the center of town? How far would you say it is?"

"Yeah, fifteen blocks," said Uncle Ben. "She shouldn't go alone."

"I'm not going with her." Ruth put her glasses back on her nose. "I came here to relax on the beach, not look at postcards in tourist shops."

"I can go on my own," said Frankie. She didn't want Ruth with her anyway. "Fifteen blocks is not that far."

"There are some shady characters around here," Uncle Ben warned. "Atlantic City is only a few miles north."

"Bunny, you don't know your way around," said Ruth.

"The house is 42 Sea Line Avenue," replied Frankie. "I make a left on Oceanview and it's a straight shot to where the shops are. I went to the supermarket with Uncle Paul, remember?"

Ruth pursed her lips. "I don't think it's a good idea."

"What do you think is gonna happen? I'm not getting in a car with any strange men. I have a cell phone."

"It's not a town we know," said Ruth. "I don't want to argue about this."

"But what do you think will happen?"

"I don't want to get into it."

"How do you think I cross the street when I'm at Alabaster, huh?"

"Bunny Rabbit."

10

"Because I cross the street when you're not there, Mom. News flash."

Uncle Paul spoke. "Let her go, Ruth. I let Paulie Junior go in last year when he was only twelve and he was fine."

"See?" Frankie turned to her mother.

"Stay out of it, Paul," snapped Ruth. "Don't make my life difficult."

"You let Paulie Junior walk into town and not me? Paulie Junior still picks his nose. That is such a double standard."

"It is not," Ruth answered. "What Paul does with Paulie Junior is up to him, and what I do with you is up to me."

"You're treating me like a baby."

"No, I'm not, Bunny," Ruth said. "I am treating you like a very attractive, still very young, teenage girl."

"With no brain."

"With maybe not the best judgment," said Ruth.

"Since when do I have bad judgment?"

"Since you want to go to town fifteen blocks away when we don't know the area and you're wearing a string bikini." Ruth was cross now. "I wish I'd never let you go shopping for suits with Zada. Really, Frankie, you're wearing hardly any clothes, you go into town, you get lost, what do you think is gonna happen?"

"I'd call you on the cell."

11

"That's not my point."

"So what—if I were unattractive, you would let me go?" Frankie asked.

"Don't start that."

"How 'bout I stop by the house and put on a dress?"

"Frankie."

"If I were a boy, then would you let me?"

"You want to spoil the last day of our vacation with a fight?" snapped Ruth. "Is that what you want?"

"No."

"So stop talking back. Leave it alone and enjoy the beach."

"Fine. I'll go down the boardwalk." Frankie stood and shoved her feet into her flip-flops, grabbed the bag where her wallet was, and stalked across the sand.

"Be back in an hour!" called Ruth. "Call me on my cell if you're going to be late."

Frankie didn't answer.

It wasn't that she wanted postcards—or even that she wanted to go to town so much. It wasn't that Ruth had too many rules, either; or that Paulie Junior got to go on his own last year.

The problem was that to them—to Uncle Ben and her mother, and maybe even to Uncle Paul—Frankie was Bunny Rabbit.

Not a person with intelligence, a sense of direction,

and the ability to use a cell phone. Not a person who could solve a problem.

Not even a person who could walk fifteen blocks all by herself without getting run over by a car.

To them, she was Bunny Rabbit.

Innocent.

In need of protection.

Inconsequential.

A half hour later and two hundred yards down the boardwalk, Frankie was shivering in that string bikini. She'd eaten half a chocolate frozen custard before the sky had clouded over. Now the cone was giving her chills, but it had cost nearly five dollars and she couldn't bring herself to throw it away.

Her hands felt sticky and she wished she'd brought a sweatshirt.

"You gonna eat that?"

Frankie turned. Sitting on the edge of the board-walk with his feet dangling was a husky, sandy-haired boy, about seventeen years old. His small, friendly eyes squinted against the wind, and his nose was dotted with freckles.

"It's too cold."

"Can I have it?"

Frankie stared at him. "Didn't your mama teach you not to beg?"

The boy laughed. "She tried. But it appears I can't be trained."

"You really want a frozen custard some stranger has licked? That's disgusting."

"So it is," said the boy, reaching out his hand for the cone. "But only a little." Frankie let him have it. He stuck out his tongue and touched the custard. Then he squashed the top down into the cone, putting his whole mouth over it. "See? Now the worst is over and it's just my own spit. And I have a frozen custard for free."

"Uh-huh."

"You'd be surprised what people will do if you ask them."

"I didn't want it anyhow."

"I know." The boy grinned. "But you might have given it to me even if you did want it. Just because I asked. Don't you think?"

"That's a lot of chutzpah you've got there. Don't let it weigh you down."

"I hate to see food go to waste. I'm always hungry." The boy raised his eyebrows, and suddenly Frankie felt that her mother was right about the string bikini. It was not enough clothing.

She was standing in what was basically her underwear, talking to a strange boy.

What was actually smaller than her underwear.

To a cute boy.

"What grade are you in?" she asked. To talk about something ordinary.

"Going into twelfth. And you?"

"Tenth."

"You're an infant!"

"Don't say that."

"All right." He shrugged. "But I thought you were older."

"Well, I'm not."

"What school do you go to?"

"It's in northern Massachusetts." Frankie said what Alabaster students always say, to avoid the ostentation of admitting they go to one of the most expensive, most academically rigorous private schools in the nation. The way Yale students inevitably say they go to school in New Haven.

"Where?" the boy asked.

"Why, do you know northern Massachusetts?"

"A little. I go to Landmark in New York City."

"Oh."

"Now you owe me. Where do you go?"

"It's called Alabaster."

"Shocker." A smile crossed the boy's face.

"What?"

"Come on. Everyone's heard of Alabaster. Exeter, Andover, Alabaster. A triumvirate of preparatory academies."

"I guess so." Frankie blushed.

"I drove down here just for the afternoon. From the city," said the boy.

"By yourself?"

He shrugged. "Yeah. I had a fight with the menstrual unit."

"The what?"

"My mom. The menstrual unit, the maternal unit, you know."

"You're mad at your mom so you're down here by yourself scrounging custard off girls?"

"Something like that."

Frankie's cell buzzed in her bag. "Speaking of. Mothers," she said. She flipped the phone open. "Mine is on the rampage."

"Where are you?" Ruth demanded. "I'm walking down the boardwalk and I don't see you anywhere."

"I'm by the custard stand. What?"

"Paulie Junior stepped on a jellyfish. We're packing up. What custard stand? There are at least five custard stands."

"Hold on." Frankie didn't want her mother to see this boy. This smart, strange boy she probably shouldn't be talking to. And she didn't want the boy to meet Ruth, either. "She's yanking my chain," she told him, and held out her hand. "I gotta go."

His hand felt warm and solid in hers. "Good luck

at school," he said. "Maybe I'll see you around."

"Frankie? Frankie! Who are you talking to?" Ruth's voice barked from the phone.

"You're not going to see me around," laughed Frankie, beginning to walk away. "You live in New York City."

"Maybe I do and maybe I don't," called the boy. "You did say Alabaster, right?"

"That's right."

"Okay, then."

"I gotta go." Frankie put the phone back to her ear. "Mom, I'm on my way back. I'll be there in five. Will you please relax?"

"Good-bye!" called the boy.

Frankie shouted back: "I hope you liked the custard."

"I like vanilla better!" he called.

And when she turned to look for him again, he was gone.

OLD BOY

*F*RANKIE'S DAD, FRANKLIN, had wanted a son to name after himself. However, he did realize that since Ruth was forty-two when Frankie was born, he probably wasn't getting one. He decided that he would just name the baby girl something as close to Frank as he could get. So they named her Frances, and called her what they called her.

Senior became Senior, which suited him.

When Frankie was five, her parents had divorced. Ruth found Senior dismissive of her intellectual capacities and personal endeavors. Senior (a WASP atheist) found Ruth's observant Judaism an irritant, and felt the pressures of maintaining relationships with two young girls and a sometimes cranky wife were infringing upon the perfection of his golf game and his advancement in the medical profession (which wasn't as stellar as he wished). After separation, Ruth took the kids to live near her family in New Jersey, while Senior remained in Boston, paying monthly visits to the children—and all the boarding school bills.

Senior Banks was a doctor specializing in lung problems. Mentally, however, he was an Old Boy— more concerned with his network of Ivy League cronies than he was with the diseases of his patients. He had attended Alabaster (back when it was all male), followed by Harvard, just as *his* father had attended Alabaster followed by Harvard.

"Old Boy" means alum, but to Frankie's mind— even before her intellectual explosion sophomore year—the oxymoron was apt. Senior's boyhood days were still the largest looming factor in his conception of himself. His former schoolfellows were his closest friends. They were the people he golfed with, the people he invited for drinks, the people whose country homes he visited on vacation. They were people he recommended for jobs; people who sent him patients and asked him to sit on boards of arts organizations; people who connected him to other people. His medical practice had become considerably more profitable in the decade since his divorce from Ruth.

When Frankie was starting sophomore year, she and Ruth drove to Boston and collected Senior for the last leg of the trip. Despite his relative lack of involvement in her life, Frankie's dad wasn't going to miss a chance to stroll the old campus and remember his glory days. He and Ruth retained a tight and false goodwill as the car headed into northern Massachusetts.

As he drove, Senior was talking about skating on the pond; going to football games. "These are the best years of your life," he boomed. "Right now is when you make the friendships that are gonna last you a lifetime. These people will get you jobs, you'll get them jobs. It's a network that's going to give you opportunities, Bunny Rabbit. Opportunities."

Ruth sighed. "Senior, really. The workplace is more democratic now."

"If it's changing," Senior snorted, "why am I paying for Alabaster?"

"To get her an education?"

"I'm not paying for the education. She could get that for ten thousand less a year. I'm paying for the connections."

Frankie's mother shrugged. "I'm just saying, take a bit of the pressure off. Let Bunny find her own way."

"Hello, Mom," said Frankie from the backseat. "I can speak for myself."

Senior took a swig of coffee from a thermos. "I'm being practical, Ruth. This is how the world operates.

You get in with the club, you're in with the club, and it makes life easier. Then it's a cinch to meet the right people to get done what you want to get done in the world."

"Nepotism."

"It's not nepotism, it's how the universe operates. People hire people they know, schools admit people they know—it's natural. Frankie is forming loyalties—and people are forming loyalties to her."

"Dad, I've already been there a year. You're talking like I've never been to the place."

"Sophomore year is when it really began to happen for me."

Frankie thought: Poor Senior. He has no life. Just a memory of a life. It's pitiful.

And then she thought: I have no friends at Alabaster that I like anywhere near so much as Senior still likes his friends from high school.

Maybe it's me who's pitiful.

And then she thought: His whole clubby thing is dumb.

And then she thought: I'd like to go to Harvard.

And then she thought—because this was the thing she'd been thinking about for most of the drive to Alabaster: I wonder if Matthew Livingston will notice me this year.

ALABASTER

*I*NFORMATION AS TO the locale and setting of Alabaster, its course requirements, and the sports activities required therein will be given in these pages solely on a need-to-know basis. It is of no relevance to the understanding of either the Loyal Order of the Basset Hounds, the Fish Liberation Society, or any of the other spurious organizations that committed the so-called crimes at Alabaster, that Frankie Landau-Banks took modern dance and played ultimate Frisbee, though she did. It does not matter that her elective was initially Latin because her father thought she should take it. And it is of no concern how she decorated her dorm room.

It is crucial, however, to understand this: Frankie Landau-Banks was and still is, in many ways, an ordinary girl. She liked clothes and was glad to have grown enough over the summer to necessitate a large school shopping trip. She bought copies of *In Touch* magazine at the drugstore and remembered silly facts about celebrities. She giggled in a goofy way when she was amused or embarrassed. She felt awkward around popular people, and couldn't figure out whether she was good-looking or freakishly ugly, because she often felt both within the space of an hour. Starting her sophomore year, she missed her sister, worried about her geometry class, and avoided Porter (the sophomore Spy Club member and lacrosse player who had been her boyfriend October through May of the previous year) in favor of pining after boys who were older than she was and unaware of her existence.

Namely, Matthew Livingston.

Other facts about Alabaster that are of actual importance to this chronicle:
1. Frankie's roommate, Trish, was a freckled, horsey blonde who'd spent the first half of her summer doing Outward Bound and the second half on Nantucket helping out in a stable. She was one of those people who is friendly to everyone, though not especially close to anyone besides her boyfriend, Artie. Trish was interested in psychology, debate, and baking; she played lacrosse and field hockey

and seemed destined to have a house in Kenne-
bunkport. Her teeth seemed like rather more teeth
than belonged in her mouth, although all of them
were straight and white.

2. Artie, Trish's boyfriend, was a member of the Audio
Visual Technology Club (AVT), which meant that
he carried keys to quite a number of buildings on
campus.

3. Alabaster was fully wired—and all the dorms had
wireless networks. Every student had a laptop
(included in the cost of tuition) and an Alabaster
e-mail address.

4. The Alabaster campus, like that of any preparatory
academy that funnels students into Ivy League
schools, had many, many buildings, most of which
are of no interest. However, take note of these
few:

  a. an old and largely neglected theater, eclipsed by
  b. a newly built arts complex;
  c. a founder's house museum;
  d. a chapel with large stained-glass windows
     featuring the crucifixion of Jesus Christ, several
     images of the Virgin Mary, and a number of
     saints, in which was held a mandatory morning
     assembly at the start of each week;
  e. an old gymnasium (now empty and blocked
     off as it awaited renovation);

f. a new gymnasium with a state-of-the-art rock-climbing wall; and

g. the Hazelton library, the architectural jewel of the campus, which featured a large and shiny dome on top.

5. In the main building, as well as in several other prominent locations, pompous oil paintings of past headmasters, distinguished teachers, literary figures, and board presidents hung with imposing and slightly ridiculous grandeur. All of the subjects were men.

6. And last: many of the buildings, built in the late nineteenth century, were connected by steam tunnels—utility tunnels intended for the maintenance of heating pipes that run underneath the ground. These tunnels were locked, and student access to them was explicitly forbidden by the administration. But there wouldn't be a story here if there weren't a way of getting in.

THE GEEK CLUB CONGLOMERATE

A TELLING ANECDOTE ABOUT Frankie
Landau-Banks:

In October of her freshman year,
the Chess Club, the Spy Club, the Science Olympiad,
the Horticulture Club, the Role-players, and the
Geography Bowl, plus a few others, had banded
together for the sake of their relatively limited memberships. They called themselves the Geek Club
Conglomerate, pooled their money, and decided to
have a party. The party was partly a membership
drive—trying to build the sparse attendance in most of
these extracurricular activities—but primarily it was a
social event. There was to be a DJ, corn chips, onion
dip, warm soda, and possibly a disco ball.

A slightly late invitation to participate in the

Conglomerate was issued to the Debate Club, of which Frankie was already a member, and naturally, the Debate Club members debated whether or not they wanted to accept membership. They didn't consider themselves geeky, and were not, in fact, universally considered geeky. Debaters had a status akin to that of people in student government—if you were really cool, you probably wouldn't bother; but participating didn't automatically connote social awkwardness.

Regarding the party, some had argued that debating was indeed geeky. They should embrace the geek factor of their chosen activity. If you called it "forensics" instead of "debate" it most certainly sounded geeky. Anyway, the only way to have any armature against the accusation of geekiness was to reinvent the term, so that *geek* and *chic* were one and the same, as they were in some sections of Silicon Valley, no doubt.

"We've got to replace geek bleak with geek chic," one proponent actually argued, while another pointed out that fighting the accusation by loudly proclaiming oneself ungeeky was certainly the geekiest thing anyone could do. He then explained that he was using "geekiest" in its pejorative sense only in that last part of his final sentence, as he hoped (but dared not assume) his fellow club members understood.

The dissenters argued that to jeopardize the precarious coolness of the Debate Club would undermine the social standing of its various members. Allying them to members of the Geography Bowl, who were notorious nose-pickers and flatulents, would cause a downslide in the collective morale of the debate team members, possibly even leading the more socially glamorous of them to depart the team so as to avoid membership in the Conglomerate. With several of its leaders decamped, the dissenters claimed, the debate team would suffer. It would lose the competitions it had traditionally won, its ranking would slide, and its members would fail to get into top colleges. The whole thing would go to hades in an alligator purse.

Frankie, then only a fledgling member of the team, had spoken up and ended the argument. "We're forgetting the two key points," she said after motioning that she wanted to speak.

"And what are they?" asked Zada, who was, as club president, acting as moderator.

"First," Frankie said, "if our stated goal here is to maintain or increase the social standing of the Debate Club, we need to think of ourselves as politicians."

"And?"

"There's a tremendous amount of damage a bunch of scorned geeks can do once they've formed a conglomerate. We would be well-advised not to irritate them if we have any pretensions to social dominance."

There was a moment of silence.

"We shouldn't piss them off," explained Frankie, "because who knows what they'll do now that they've united."

More silence. Then Zada said, "Good point. What's the second?"

"There's a party. Lots of people we know are going to it. And we're invited."

"So?"

"So. Do we want to go? I, for one, would like to go to the party."

There was a quick vote, and when it was over, the Alabaster debaters had formally joined the Geek Club Conglomerate.

Walking out of that room was the happiest moment of Frankie Landau-Banks's freshman year.

At the party, Frankie met Porter Welsch from the Spy Club and danced with him. The members of the Spy Club had pretensions to technological wizardry such as surveillance equipment, fingerprinting, and metal detectors, but the reality was that among them they owned nothing more than a pair of binoculars and one really small camera, and most of their time was spent reading and discussing the work of John le Carré and Frederick Forsyth. There were only four of them anyway.

Porter was, at age fifteen, already six foot three.

He had floppy black hair and a heft to his frame that was uncommon in even radically tall boys of his age. He wasn't much of a dancer, but he knew it, and the faces he pulled when he danced gave him a perpetually startled look—as if he were, at regular intervals, surprised to find himself dancing. And with a girl, too.

Frankie already knew who Porter was, of course. His father was head of a power company that was exceedingly profitable, yet frequently written up in *The New York Times* for questionable business practices. (People at Alabaster know this kind of thing about one another's families.) There had been a trial several years back that ended in a hung jury, and other suits were pending—but Mr. Welsch had remained a prosperous, if notorious, CEO. Porter was the youngest of three children, all of whom attended Alabaster; his sister Jeannie was two years ahead of him.

Porter asked Frankie if she wanted to study algebra with him in the library the next evening, and she said yes.

They laughed over their homework (eighth-grade stuff). They both liked reading and strawberry Mentos. Before Frankie knew it, Porter was walking her back to her dorm and they had kissed beneath a streetlamp.

She liked him. He was big. He seemed like more of a man than the other boys his age. She liked his messy dorm room stacked with piles of paperbacks.

She also liked watching him on the lacrosse field, where he was a star. She couldn't quite believe he liked *her*, since at that point she looked very much like an uncomfortable kid, all gawky elbows and too-long legs, startling jaw and frizzy curls; but Porter said he thought she was funny, and that she had beautiful eyes.

It was nice to have a boyfriend. And though they weren't "in love" and no love was ever discussed, Frankie and Porter went out for many months. She went to his lacrosse games. He attended her debates. They sent each other adorable e-mails and spent every Saturday night together. She met his family when they came on Parents Day (and was, in fact, surprised to find his dad balding and jovial, since Porter had talked about him with such revulsion). They held hands in the movies and sat together in the caf. They were the longest-standing couple in the freshman class.

Until mid-May.

On May 19th, Frankie walked in on Porter fooling around with Bess Montgomery, a junior girl with a heart-shaped face and a taste for tall boys.

Frankie wept.

Porter made excuses.

Frankie said she never wanted to speak to him again.

She thought he'd come knocking on her door with a mouth full of apologies, but he never did.

MATTHEW

O N THE SECOND DAY of school sophomore year, before classes actually started, Frankie caught sight of Matthew across the quad.

He was a senior. A dimpled chin, a ready smile, unruly dark hair, black-rimmed glasses that contrasted with his wide, wide shoulders. Matthew was a Livingston, meaning his father owned newspapers in Boston, Philadelphia, and Burlington. His mother was a celebrated socialite and fund-raiser for the Juvenile Diabetes Foundation and other worthy liberal charities. His family went back to Jamestown—but you'd never know it from his clothes. Like the other students at Alabaster, Matthew wore none of his wealth on his back. Old chinos and a thin red T-shirt with a stain on the stomach, ancient sneakers, and the same backpack

Frankie knew he'd carried last year. He was editor of the school paper and a member of the heavy eight on the crew team, pulling the key fifth seat. More important, he was known for organizing late-night parties and hijacking golf carts.

When Frankie saw Matthew sophomore year, she was biking over to the new gymnasium to meet her roommate, Trish, for a swim. She caught sight of him walking down the path and was so engrossed in watching the way his hips rolled underneath the waist of his ratty khakis that—dumb, girly—she lost control of the bicycle, spun onto the grass, and fell over.

Ow. Her leg was scraped up, and she'd made a fool of herself. Frankie felt like an idiot—until Matthew Livingston (Matthew Livingston!) ran over and came to her aid.

Then she felt like a genius. And wished her hair wasn't frizzing in the September heat. Because he was here, standing over her, looking concerned. Matthew Livingston!

"Are you okay?" Matthew pulled the bike off her and tossed it to one side like it weighed nothing.

Frankie looked down at her leg. It was bleeding around the ankle. She was relieved to find something reasonably clever coming out of her mouth: "They say it's like riding a bicycle," she quipped, "but I guess it isn't."

Matthew smiled. "Did you get new legs for the new school year?"

"That's it," Frankie answered. "They're not working smoothly yet." It was surprisingly easy to talk to him. Last year she had been unable to say two words when he was around. "Now look," Frankie said, pouting. "I've got them all dirty."

He held out a hand and helped her up. "You're a freshman here, right? I'm Matthew Livingston."

"No." She kept her face calm, but inside she was all dismay. He didn't remember her.

"What?" Matthew was asking.

"I'm a sophomore. I was here last year."

"Really?"

"I'm Frankie. Zada Landau-Banks's little sister."

"I didn't know Zada had a sister."

Actually, Zada had introduced Frankie to Matthew more than once. Frankie had even sat with Matthew (and many others) for dinner in the cafeteria. Twice. One time, to illustrate a point, he had collected corncobs from everyone at his table and built a model of the Parthenon using plastic trays, the cobs, and small juice cups, only to abandon the project three-quarters done, saying, "Oh, this is way too disgusting, I'll just have to lose the argument."

The other time, late in the spring, he and his friend Dean had talked about driving cross-country with someone named Alpha. They were planning a road trip from Boston to San Francisco, with stops at greasy spoon diners all across the nation. "We're going to search out the perfect piece of apple pie," explained Matthew.

"Or cherry," added Dean.

"Or cherry. Or lemon meringue. Some seriously good pie, is what I'm saying. The plan is to start school in the fall at least ten pounds heavier than we are now."

"We're gonna film it, too," said Dean. "Like a whole documentary of us eating pie across America."

"If we survive."

"Yeah. Alpha is a madman driver. Did we tell you he's trying to organize a drag race at that school, wherever he is?"

"Who's Alpha?" Frankie asked.

Zada shook her head as if to say, Keep quiet, I'll explain later, and asked, "Why does he want to drag race?"

"He's been watching *Rebel Without a Cause*. You know how he is, he likes to stir up trouble. Anyway, these New York guys, they're like, What, are you gonna drag race us in that Volvo? Because he's got that Volvo his mom got him, used, and Alpha's all, Yes, I'm gonna drag race you in the Volvo! And then they saw him drive it and now they're terrified, because Alpha in a Volvo is like anyone else in a freaking race car."

Zada rolled her eyes. "What a nimrod."

Dean laughed. "He's not really gonna drag race them, though. You know Alpha, he's all talk."

"He's still a scary-ass driver," said Matthew. "So we'll either come back chubby or come back dead, but either way there are gonna be changes next year."

"And we'll have a movie of it!" added Dean. "Whatever it is."

"You guys are certifiable." Zada had laughed and stood to bus her tray. Frankie followed.

"And you love us for it!" Matthew had called after her.

"Maybe I do and maybe I don't," Zada yelled over her shoulder.

"Where's Zada gone?" Matthew now asked Frankie, as she pulled her bike up.

"Berkeley. Broke my dad's heart she didn't go to Harvard."

"She got into Harvard?" Matthew looked impressed. Frankie loved the way his eyes crinkled. "Who wouldn't pick Harvard?"

Frankie shrugged. "She's not into all that stuff. She wanted to go somewhere more relaxed, farther from home. He's intense, my dad."

Matthew nodded. "So, do you need someone to show you around?"

"I told you, I'm not new. You just don't remember me from last year." She felt mildly injured.

"I know you're not new."

"Oh."

"But . . ."

"But what?"

"Do you need someone to show you around, anyway?"

He was flirting with her.

Matthew Livingston, whom Frankie had liked ever since that dumb corncob Parthenon, even when she was dating Porter; Matthew, who made her blood rush whenever she saw him; Matthew, with those wide shoulders and those ice-chip cheekbones under the black frames of his glasses—he was flirting with her.

"Help me, help me. I'm bleeding and I can't find the new gymnasium!" she cried, draping her wrist over her forehead dramatically.

"That's more like it," said Matthew, and he walked her where she had to go, making up lies about all the landmarks on the way.

Alpha

Alpha's real name was Alessandro Tesorieri, but no one ever called him that anymore. Within two days of his freshman year (he was now a senior) his alpha dog status was so obvious that someone made a joke of it—and he had been Alpha ever since.

Alpha's mother had never been married to his father. When Alessandro was only one, his single mother, Elena, met a handsome jewelry-store magnate and allowed herself to be supported by him for years—although they never lived together. The boy had been raised in luxury. The best schools, the Fifth Avenue penthouse, a house in the country. The couple stayed together for more than a decade until the summer after Alpha's sophomore year at Alabaster—when the magnate left Elena for a younger woman. He let Alpha's mother keep the penthouse he'd bought her, with its dead-expensive monthly maintenance, and disappeared from their lives.

Without paying school fees for the coming year.

So Alpha spent his junior year in a New York City public school, thereby acquiring legendary status at Alabaster. But despite rumored triumphs at drag racing, cockfighting, and Foosball, the boy was miserable. Without consulting Elena, come spring he sent a letter to Headmaster Richmond at Alabaster, explaining the situation (the penthouse hadn't sold and Elena's dilettante interior-design work didn't bring in much), and requesting to return for his senior year—on scholarship.

He was hailed as a conquering hero. Frankie heard the full Alpha story from Matthew that day as he walked her to the pool. And though she didn't say anything—she could tell Matthew wanted to ramble on about his friend without being questioned— Frankie thought it sounded more like a return with tail firmly between legs than a triumph.

Is an alpha dog still an alpha dog if you move him away from his pack? she wondered. In a new pack, would he jockey himself up to the alpha dog position, or would he become the runt, the zed, the unloved stranger? And if he had become alpha dog in this new pack, as everyone assumed Tesorieri had, would he really want to return to the old one?

"Why'd he come back?" Frankie asked Matthew. They were standing outside the new gymnasium, looking through Plexiglas windows at the floor-to-ceiling rock-climbing wall. Frankie was late for swimming by now. She knew Trish was probably kick-boarding back and forth without her. But she also knew Trish would forgive her, since her trespass involved Matthew Livingston.

"Couldn't live without me," Matthew joked.

"But if he had so much freedom, like you said? Running cockfights on the Lower East Side? He doesn't sound like a guy who'd want to come back to boarding school. Where like every second of our day is scheduled, and someone's always watching everything we do."

"For a guy like Alpha, rules exist for breaking. He likes a challenge," said Matthew, looking at Frankie, not at the rock-climbers. "I'm thinking Alpha and his Volvo and his pet rooster cakewalked all over that city. He had to come back so he'd have something to really *do*."

Frankie shook her head. "He came back because going to Alabaster will get him into a good college, right?"

"Probably," Matthew admitted. "Whoa, speak of the devil."

"What?"

"That's him." Matthew banged his fist on the Plexiglas window. "Alpha!"

"He's on the rock wall?"

"He's on the freaking wall. Like he appeared out of thin air. I swear he wasn't there when we were looking before, was he?"

Frankie shrugged and followed Matthew as he ran into the new gymnasium and down a long series of steps to the bottom of the wall. Dean was belaying Alpha as he rappelled from the top. Matthew and Frankie stood and watched.

Frankie had imagined Alpha Tesorieri as a five-o'clock-shadowed Italian bad boy wearing black leather and driving a motorcycle.

But he wasn't.

He was—the boy from the Jersey Shore.

The one who had scrounged her frozen custard off her.

The one who had said, "It appears I can't be trained."

The one who had said, "I'm always hungry."

Medium height and sandy haired, with a barrel chest and a baby face, Alpha wasn't looking at Frankie. "Arggggh!" he yelled when he hit the ground. "That wall just kicked me from here to Tuscaloosa. I am hereby declaring war on that wall,

41

Dean. Do you hear me? That wall is toast by the end of the semester."

"You're out of shape, dog." Dean chuckled.

"It's like I was lugging every dang coconut pie I ate this summer up that freaking wall." Alpha threw himself extravagantly on the floor mats, face down. "I am just going to lie here and commune with the foot smell," he announced. "That's all I'm really good for at this point."

"Dog, Livingston's here with some girl."

Alpha popped up. "Livingston!" he cried, rushing at Matthew. "Let me wipe my sweat on you as a gesture of fraternal love!" He rubbed his wet pink face on Matthew's T-shirt. "How was the Vineyard?"

"Sheep everywhere, dog," said Matthew. "Sheep as far as the eye can see. And then when there's no more sheep, oxen."

"I love oxen!" Alpha's eye flitted to Frankie and back again. Did he recognize her?

"You *would* love oxen." Matthew smirked.

"No really, they are so butch. Wouldn't you love to be an oxen? An ox, whatever?" asked Alpha.

"An ox," said Matthew. "That's the singular. And no, thank you, I would not."

"Who are you?" Alpha turned to Frankie. "Call me Alpha."

"This is Frankie," Matthew said.

So he didn't recognize her. Frankie held out her hand and Alpha shook it. It was wet with perspiration, but she remembered the way it felt.

"Sorry about the sweat. Now I've wiped my sweat all over you; we're bonded for life. Did you know that?"

She laughed.

"Seriously. I only do it to people I like. You saw me do it to Livingston, right? It's like blood brothers."

Matthew fake-kicked Alpha. "Don't talk to her like that, she'll never hang out with us again."

"Oh, so are you with Livingston now?" Alpha asked.

"We just met, dog," laughed Matthew. "Lay off."

"He's the handsomest one of us, though, don't you think?" Alpha said, wiping his brow. "He's like Adonis or whatever."

Frankie couldn't deny it. Instead she said, "I think I met you at the beach a few weeks ago."

Alpha squinted at her, the same way he'd done the afternoon they first met. "I'm from New York City. No beach there, unless it's Coney Island. But hey, any girl of Livingston's is a friend of mine. Dean, meet Frankie, by the way."

Dean walked over. "Hi, Frankie."

"She's Zada's little sister," explained Matthew. "You remember Zada?"

"You a freshman?" Dean asked.

"Sophomore," Frankie answered.

"Funny," Dean said. "I swear I've never set eyes on you in my life. I would remember you. I know I would."

When Matthew hadn't remembered her, Frankie had felt mildly pleased to have changed so radically that he didn't even know she was the same girl; when Alpha hadn't, she'd felt small. Just another girl he'd chatted up on the beach and then forgotten. But when Dean didn't remember her, she got angry. "I ate lunch with you more than once," she said, giving him an even stare. "Because I used to sit with my sister. We had a conversation one day about Pirates of the Caribbean."

"The ride or the movie?"

"The ride. The old ride versus the updated ride."

"I don't remember."

"I was telling you how there were hidden Mickey Mouses and shadows of Pluto on the old ride? How Zada and I looked them up on the Web before we went?"

Dean shook his head.

"The giant rock that looks like Goofy?"

He shrugged, and Frankie wondered how he could possibly have forgotten a conversation like that.

"He's a nimrod for not remembering," said Matthew, as if he hadn't done something similar himself. "Say you're a nimrod, Dean."

"Oh, I'm a nimrod. Ask anyone you see."

"Alpha," Frankie said, turning, "is Dean a nimrod?"

"Of course, Frankie-that-I-sweated-on. But he also has no short-term memory. He's obliterated half his brain cells with that contraption he keeps in his room."

Dean nodded. "It's true. My cognitive functioning is noticeably impaired."

"Except for the straight-A average." Matthew socked Dean on the arm.

"Except nothing," answered Dean. "It's all smoke and mirrors. Pay no attention to the man behind the curtain!"

Frankie couldn't stay angry, though she was sure Dean was lying about not remembering her. How could she be mad when they were so completely undignified? Magnificently silly. Willing to send themselves up at the slightest opportunity, prostrate themselves, admit to frailties. Dean openly mocked himself and acted almost ashamed of his straight-A marks. Alpha wasn't embarrassed that he'd barely made it up the easy course on the rock wall; he sweated on people and made fun of his own physique. And Matthew—well, she couldn't have been mad at Matthew, anyway.

These guys, they were so sure of their places in life—so deeply confident of their merit and their future—they didn't need any kind of front at all.

The Ladies

"IT WAS THE SAME GUY from the beach, I'd swear on my mother's grave," Frankie finished as she and Trish kick-boarded the length of the pool.

Trish was the roommate, you'll recall. "No way," she said, breathing hard as she kicked.

"It was him," said Frankie.

"The one who took your custard? Whose name you never got?"

"Yes."

"And did you fall into each other's arms?"

"He didn't remember me."

"Get out."

"None of them remembered me, Trish."

"You're kidding."

"Not Dean, and not Matthew, not this Alpha guy. It's like I'm invisible."

"Like you *were* invisible," corrected Trish. "And now you're not."

"Because my chest filled out? Come on. They have got to look at girls' faces every once in a while. Otherwise how are they going to recognize anyone?"

Trish laughed. "I'm betting that if all of us started padding or wearing minimizers, the boys of this school would be completely confused and unable to identify at least half of the female population. Haven't you seen the way they always talk to your chest?"

"No."

"Well, you didn't have that much chest last year, no offense. But that's what they do. They talk to the Ladies. If you know what I mean."

"It can't be all about the Ladies."

"Yes, it can."

"Be serious."

Trish hauled herself out of the pool. "Okay, you're right. Matthew didn't remember you because he's a big man on campus. All he cares about are the people in his own circle, and he's oblivious to everything else, even when it's right in front of his nose—unless he sees a girl he's attracted to."

"Oh, I don't think he's like that."

"Whatever. Dean, though: you're right. I think he's lying, because that Dean guy is always trying to make himself feel important. He acts like he doesn't remember you because that makes him feel big—it gives him the upper hand in the conversation."

"But why does he even need it?"

"Because Matthew obviously likes you, that's why. And Dean is threatened by anything that takes Matthew away from him."

"Good thing your mom is a shrink."

Trish squeezed water out of her hair. "It is good. Now, on to the third one. There is no way that Alpha guy wouldn't remember you. It was only two weeks ago you guys were flirting on the beach."

"I even mentioned how we'd met, but he blew it off. Like it wasn't him." Frankie was out of the water now, too. She rubbed her legs with a towel.

"Why would he do that?"

"I don't know."

"But the guy at the beach knew you went to Alabaster, yes? So if this is the same guy, then he knows you're the same girl."

"I know." They walked into the sauna and lay down in the hot, cedar smell.

"Are you upset?" asked Trish. "Do you like him?"

"I would . . ." Frankie considered. "I might . . . But I was with Matthew Livingston."

49

Trish stood and rearranged her towel. "That's why the Alpha guy pretended he didn't remember," she finally said, stretching back out.

"Why?"

"Because you were with Matthew."

"So?"

"So Matthew was talking to the Ladies, and when Matthew talks to the Ladies, all the competition might as well retire."

"Grodie."

"I'm just saying."

"That Alpha backed down to defer to Matthew?"

"Matthew's . . . well, let me put it this way," said Trish. "If I didn't have Artie, I wouldn't say no. There isn't a girl at Alabaster who'd say no. He's Matthew Livingston. So the Alpha guy had prior claim, but he backed off when Matthew got hold of you."

"You're making me sound like a piece of meat."

"No, of course you're not. I'm living vicariously."

"How?"

"It would be fun to have guys fighting over me. I'm not even sixteen and already I'm, like, married."

"It's not even clear if he likes me," said Frankie.

"Which one?"

"Either one. Matthew."

"I don't think Alpha was talking to you to get your custard."

Frankie stretched herself. "Maybe he's not so alpha after all, if he backed off like that."

"Is what I'm saying," said Trish.

THE PANOPTICON

RANKIE SAW MATTHEW in the caf several times the next week at a table full of senior boys; but it was impossible for a sophomore to walk over to a senior table and just say hello in front of everyone. Once, he passed her outside, running in his soccer practice clothes—a pair of cleats swinging in one hand. "Late!" he'd grinned in explanation, looking over his shoulder and loping off in the direction of the playing fields.

Oh, he had great legs.

Had he not been interested, after all? Frankie wondered as she watched him go. Was she too young for him?

Had he stopped liking her when she'd talked back to Dean about the Pirates of the Caribbean ride?

All week she tried not to think of him, and actually studied for her classes. On the weekend she went to town with Trish and Artie, and played an ultimate Frisbee game.

At the start of the second week of classes, however, Frankie switched out of Latin and into an elective called Cities, Art, and Protest that sounded like more fun. The class was taught by a teacher named Ms. Jensson. She was new to Alabaster and wore beaded cardigan sweaters and unusual skirts. She had a master's from Columbia in art history and told everyone she'd come to Alabaster to escape New York City—but then here she was, spending all her time discussing it in class. So ironic.

It was the first time Frankie had ever taken a course that couldn't be described in a single word: French. Biology. Latin. History. Ms. Jensson explained various ways of conceptualizing cities and how organically developing cities contrasted with smaller, more deliberately planned environments such as Alabaster's own campus. The students read architecture criticism, a history of Paris, and studied the panopticon—a kind of prison designed by late eighteenth/early nineteenth-century philosopher Jeremy Bentham, which was never actually built.

The architecture of Bentham's panopticon was created to allow a watchman to look at all his prisoners without the prisoners knowing whether or not they were being observed—making them feel as if they were constantly being watched by an omniscient being.

In other words, everyone in the panopticon knew they could be watched at all times, so in the end, only minimal watching actually needed to happen. The panopticon would create a sense of paranoia so pervasive that its inhabitants became practically self-governing.

Ms. Jensson then had the students read an excerpt from a book called *Discipline and Punish*, in which Michel Foucault uses the idea of the panopticon as a metaphor for Western society and its emphasis on normalization and observation. Meaning, we live our lives in places that operate like the panopticon. Schools. Hospitals. Factories. Office buildings. Even the streets of the city.

Someone is watching you.

Or, someone is *probably* watching you.

Or, you *feel* like someone's watching you.

So you follow the rules whether someone's watching you or not.

You start to think that whomever is watching you is larger than life. That the watcher *knows* stuff about you that you never told anyone.

Even if the watcher is someone dumb like a boarding-school headmaster.

Or an eighteen-year-old schoolboy.

Or a fifteen-year-old girl *pretending* to be an eighteen-year-old schoolboy.

It's a systematic paranoia. Like, when you have that creepy sense that your dad knows you drank that beer, even though you drank it four days ago and there's no evidence whatsoever that he knows.

Or when you are alone in your house, and you go to use the toilet and lock the door behind you anyway.

Or when you have a new boyfriend and you're alone in your room and you pick your nose—and then you think how grodie that was, and how somehow your boyfriend must have been able to see you and he's going to dump your slimy, nose-picking self as soon as you see him next. And you can also kind of hear your grandmother's voice in your head, reminding you to use a tissue. And that horrible queen-bee popular girl—you can hear her nasty voice back in the fifth grade when she caught you wiping a booger on the underside of your desk, calling you "booger eater" for half the school year, even though obviously if you were eating your boogers you wouldn't have been wiping them on the desk in the first place.

So it's not that you either pick your nose because you want to pick it, or you don't pick your nose because it's germy. It's that you are having a mental conversation with all the forces that could be watching you and condemning you for your nose-picking (potential or actual)—even though rationally you know that no one can see you.

That's the panopticon.

Cities, Art, and Protest was so much better than Latin. Frankie did all her reading early.

THE INVITATIONS

RANKIE FIRST NOTICED the pale blue envelopes in her morning history class a week and a half into the school year. Star Allan, a sophomore who lived on Frankie's hall, sat with her friend Claudia, comparing notes.

Star was petite. A crew team coxswain. A brash, loud voice. A ponytail so long and swingy, Frankie wondered it didn't topple her backward. A brain the size of a corn kernel. "Did you get one of these?" Star called across the table, flashing her envelope and the matching card within.

Star was going out with Dean, Frankie knew.

"No."

"Did you?" Star asked Trish.

"What is it?"

"Oh, you'll know if you're supposed to know!" sang Star. "If you don't have one, I can't show you mine!"

Later, eating lunch in the caf, Frankie couldn't help but notice pale blue envelopes in the hands and pockets of several popular seniors. And when she looked over toward the corner table where such people always sat, Matthew, Dean, Alpha, and their pack were leaning back in their chairs, the cards scattered across the table.

Frankie checked her mailbox after lunch, but there was nothing inside except a flyer about Saturday water polo.

That night, Frankie was alone in the library. She had signed out of the dorm to go to a study session for tomorrow's biology test, and when the session ended, Frankie went down in the 8000 section of the stacks to look for something fun to read.

It was cold among the metal shelves in the basement of the library, and there was a smell of dusty paper. Frankie was looking for a book by P. G. Wodehouse, having read *Something Fresh* over the summer; but she hadn't bothered to look him up in the catalog, and so was wandering through the W's, misremembering the spelling of his name (pronounced Woodhouse), and wondering whether she should bother going upstairs to do a computer search or just see if there was anything decent to read that would be easier to find—when she heard voices.

At the end of the long line of bookshelves was a row of study carrels, each a fluorescent-lit cubicle with a Plexiglas door and room inside for two chairs and a desk. Four senior boys—Matthew, Alpha, Dean, and Callum—were squeezed into one of them, two sitting on top of the desk and two in the chairs. The carrel was nearly soundproof, and Frankie couldn't hear what they were saying. She thought no more about it, aside from a lingering consciousness that Matthew Livingston was within several yards of her body—and wandered farther down into the W's, where she eventually found a shelf of Wodehouse stories.

She took *The Code of the Woosters* because she liked the title, and opened it, sitting down on the floor. She was involved enough to feel mildly startled when the boys opened the carrel door and their noise spilled out into the stacks.

"Gidget . . ." Matthew's friend Callum was laughing. "I can't believe you guys." Gidget was a good-looking junior who had thus far managed not to date anyone at Alabaster.

Matthew biffed Callum gently on the back of the head. "It's not charity, nimrod."

Callum asked, "What do you mean?"

"It's a reward in anticipation of future service," Matthew answered.

"Whatever."

"We're serious," said Alpha, putting his arm around Callum's shoulders. "We may need your talents later in the year."

"Okay."

"Meanwhile, you have a date on Friday with Gidget."

Matthew said, "Alpha, you are such a matchmaker."

"It's true." Frankie watched as Alpha, in the lead, walked past the aisle where she was sitting. "I love interfering in people's lives," he continued. "It provides me oodles of entertainment."

"You're a sick man, you know that?" Matthew smirked.

"They should probably institutionalize me," Alpha said philosophically. "Oh, wait. They already have!"

The panopticon, Frankie thought.

"The Alabaster prison," laughed Matthew.

"So beautifully green, so pungent, so highbrow," moaned Alpha in mock distress, "that even when the alpha dog escapes, he ends up crawling back and begging: incarcerate me!"

The boys mounted the stairs, making noise in the library like they owned it.

* * *

A minute later, Frankie heard footsteps coming back through the stacks. She looked up from her spot on the floor, and there—silhouetted against the light that shone from inside the study carrels—was Matthew.

"Hey," he said. "I thought that was you. What are you reading?"

She lifted *The Code of the Woosters* and showed it to him.

"Nice."

"Have you read it?"

"I read something by him. I forget what. Listen."

"What?" She wanted to stand, but he was right there, looking down at her, and to get up would have brought their faces uncomfortably close together.

"Did you check your mail?" Matthew asked.

"Um. This morning. Not recently."

"Well." He grinned and turned to walk back out of the library. "You should check it."

His footsteps hastened to a run, and he was gone.

Frankie left her stack of books lying on the floor and headed for the mailboxes in the main building. The lobby was deserted but for past headmasters and board presidents glowering down from paintings on the walls. Frankie stuck her tongue out at them and opened her mailbox, hands shaking.

Inside was a pale blue envelope sealed with

red sealing wax like a Victorian love letter.

"Frankie Landau-Banks," the card inside read, in glued-on letters cut from a newspaper. The rest of the words were printed on a computer and would have been the same for all recipients:

```
Tell no one you have received this
invitation. On Saturday night, ten minutes
after curfew, dress in black. Get some
alcohol if you can. Come to the golf
course. Do not be seen! Your partner in
this life of crime is—
```

And here there was a space, and letters were glued in again:

"—Matthew Livingston."

There was no signature, no hint of who had sent the invitation. Frankie flipped the card over. Nothing. She looked again at the envelope. Stamped into the red sealing wax was a line drawing of a dog with droopy ears. A basset hound.

Senior had been a Basset at Alabaster. Every couple of months he took Frankie and Zada out to a fancy Boston steak house with some old friends of his—Hank Sutton (CEO of a paper company), William

Steerforth (a high-profile lawyer), and Dr. John Montague (head of a Boston-area hospital). The men usually finished off two bottles of wine and three large steaks while Frankie and Zada ate cheese fondue. They would get silly, the Old Boys, from all the wine and animal protein—and they'd talk about the Bassets.

It was a secret society, but what precisely *for* was hard to tell. Senior's reminiscences were largely of campus escapades like posting mysterious coded messages on the message boards or sneaking out after curfew. He and his friends seemed to want Frankie and Zada to know the society existed—and that they'd been members; but they didn't want to answer any direct questions. One night as they all sat looking at the remains of a heavy meal spread out across a soiled white tablecloth, the Old Boys did admit they'd kept a record of their misdeeds in a notebook they called *The Disreputable History*. But when Frankie asked Mr. Sutton what they'd written in it, he laughed and shook his head. "Now if I told you that, it wouldn't be a secret, would it?"

"But you're telling us about the society," Frankie said, "so how big a secret can it be?"

"Secrets are more powerful when people know you've got them," said Mr. Sutton. "You show them the tiniest edge of your secret, but the rest you keep under wraps."

"Where do you keep this history?"

"Bind it tight with sticking plaster!" laughed Dr. Montague, who had drunk more than his share of the cabernet.

"Look to the west, boys!" giggled Senior.

"Oh no," moaned Mr. Steerforth. "Not that again."

"I can't believe we did that," chuckled Dr. Montague. "Look to the books, boys!"

"What do you mean?" Frankie wanted to know.

"Nothing, nothing," said Dr. Montague.

"Ignore your father and these silly fellows to my left," said Mr. Sutton. "You two charming young ladies know much more how to behave in a good restaurant than they do."

"Who's to say Frankie won't be a Basset?" asked Zada, at that time a senior, while Frankie was a freshman. "Maybe she'll join. You should tell her all about it."

Mr. Sutton laughed outright, and Mr. Steerforth said, "Sorry, Frankie, it's an all-male organization."

"You knew that, Zada," Senior scolded. "Why do you have to go giving Bunny Rabbit ideas when she'll just end up disappointed?"

"Yeah, I knew," said Zada. "I think it's dumb, that's all."

"Enough," snapped Senior.

"Who's getting dessert?" asked Dr. Montague. "I'm getting Boston cream pie."

Now Frankie looked at the basset hound seal on the edge of her envelope and wondered briefly about her father's society. It still existed, that was clear, and she wondered how it operated and what power it had on campus.

But mostly (let's be honest here) Frankie's thoughts were elsewhere. After all, Matthew Livingston— Matthew Livingston!—had finally asked her out.

The Woods

S ECURITY AT ALABASTER was lax. The feeling of being watched generated by the panoptical nature of the boarding school institution was enough to keep most of the students obeying the rules without the need for any serious levels of surveillance.

Matthew stuck a note under Frankie's dorm room door on Saturday morning, explaining that she was to take the north stairwell down to the second floor (thereby staying as far from the hall supervisor's room as possible), then cross through the lounge to the small kitchen nobody used, which had a back door onto a tiny porch with steps leading down to the Dumpsters behind the dorm. The bar across the door claimed to be alarmed, but Matthew knew that last year, at least, it never had been.

A note in Matthew's writing.

Although it said *BURN THIS* in large letters at the bottom, Frankie carried it around for half the day before setting it on fire.

She was going out with Matthew Livingston.

Late at night.

To a party he was giving with his friends.

Last year, if you'd asked her, Frankie would have said such a thing was impossible. She had been a kid, and he was almost a man. She had been nobody and he had been golden. And yet here it was, happening—as easy as, well, falling off a bicycle.

Trish hadn't been invited. Her boyfriend Artie hadn't been either. Frankie felt apologetic, but Trish waved her off. "I'm gonna be on the golf course for like two hours already Saturday. Artie wants to play. I'm not going back in the middle of the night to watch a bunch of senior guys drink beer. I hate those kinds of parties."

"Since when?" asked Frankie, stretching herself across her single bed. "Since when have you even *been* to these kinds of parties?"

"My brothers took me to some on Nantucket this summer, and I was just cold and bored, watching guys show off on the beach and get drunk."

"Weren't there any girls?"

"Yeah, there were girls, but it was—" Trish sighed.

"It was macho, somehow. I went a few times, and then I just told Topher and James I was staying home."

"What did you do instead?"

"Watched movies with the parents. Made crumbles."

"What, like berry crumbles?"

"And peach. And rhubarb."

"Really?"

"It's fun," answered Trish. "Way funner than listening to guys talk about sports and slur their words, I'll tell you that."

Frankie found her friend's attitude infuriating. By opting out of what the boys were doing in favor of a typically feminine pursuit, Trish had closed a door—the door between herself and that boys' club her brothers had on the beach. Sure, she was still invited. She could open the door again. But another summer spent making crumbles in the kitchen, and the boys would stop asking her to come out. Instead they'd expect warm dessert to be waiting for them on their return.

"Will you get up when I call you and let me back in through the kitchen?" Frankie asked, suppressing her irritation.

"Of course," said Trish. "I'll sleep with my cell."

The nights were still warm—it was only early September—so Frankie wore black cotton chinos and

a long-sleeved navy T-shirt. She put extra leave-in conditioner on her frizzy hair, and a pearly shine of pink
across her cheekbones. Matthew was waiting for her
in the woods behind the Heaton dorm, just as he said
he'd be.

"Hey," he whispered. "You made it."

She nodded.

"You got my note okay?"

"Yes."

"And did you burn it?"

"Look." Frankie held her hand up close to his face.
"Band-Aid."

"I had no idea it was going to burn so fast. What
did you write on, tissue paper?"

Matthew laughed. They were walking in the
woods that surrounded the Alabaster campus, out of
the glare of the streetlamps that lined the quad.
Frankie could see other black-clad figures traipsing
through the dark, though she couldn't tell who anyone
was.

They traveled in silence for a minute, then
Matthew took her hand—the one with the Band-Aid.
"I'm concerned about you reinjuring your hand," he
said. "For your own protection, I think I have to hold
it, to keep it safe from thorns and vicious woodland
animals."

"All right," said Frankie. "But if it feels greasy,

that's from the Neosporin I put on like half an hour ago. It's not like I'm naturally covered with grease."

"I'll keep that in mind."

"I'm not oozing pus or anything."

"Braggart."

Matthew's hand was large and comforting. Frankie felt a tingle of joy run up her arm.

"That's what I look for in a girl," Matthew went on. "I look for a someone who is not oozing pus."

She laughed.

"Seriously," he said, stroking the inside of her wrist with his other hand as they walked, "I'm glad you came out tonight. I was worried you wouldn't come."

Was he loony? He was a senior, athletic, universally considered attractive; he had a car; he would own a slew of nationally renowned newspapers one day; he had driven cross-country with his friends, eating pie and making videos. And she, Frankie—well, she didn't think badly of herself. She knew she was unusually smart in certain subjects and could regularly make her friends laugh, and she was pleased that she was now at least reasonably good-looking most days—but she was a heterosexual sophomore with no boyfriend and no social power (especially now that Zada had graduated). On what planet would a girl in her position refuse to go to a golf course party with Matthew Livingston?

Frankie's mind was starting to turn over.

She had never wanted anything so badly as she wanted Matthew to be her boyfriend. But he'd just made this statement—that he had been worried she wouldn't come—that was nearly impossible to answer with any dignity. What could she say that was most likely to get her where she wanted to be? Her synapses went into a series of calculations and evaluations that can be listed as follows:

Could say: "Here I am."

Veto. Sounds coy.

Could say: "Of course I came."

Veto. Sounds like I idolize him.

Could say: "Why wouldn't I?"

Veto. He'll feel awkward answering that question.

Could change the subject.

Veto. People like to be listened to.

Could say: "I've never been to a party on the golf course."

Veto. Too juvenile.

Could say instead: "I'm always up for a party."

Veto. Too irksome. Plus, sounds like I went to lots of parties last year, which he'll soon find out I didn't.

I need to make him laugh. And I need to unsettle him enough so that's he's not entirely certain I like him.

Golf. The golf course.

"I'm a halfway decent golfer," said Frankie after only a 2.8 second pause. "I never turn down the chance to play a few holes."

There. Matthew laughed!

Frankie glowed in satisfaction. This was better than winning a debate.

"You'll need infrared goggles," he said.

"What, you don't have?"

"Um. No."

"You expect me to play nighttime golf without serious military-level equipment?" Frankie faked a pout. "I don't think that's fair. I want this lack of tech support figured into my handicap."

Relieved that reasonably intelligible and even entertaining things were coming out of her mouth, Frankie snuck a look at Matthew. His profile was Bostonian, and his white skin glowed under his late-summer freckles. "If I'd known you were so demanding, I would have made better preparations," he said.

"Aha. So you are throwing this party."

Matthew nodded. "Me and Alpha. We matched everyone up, and Alpha got the she-wolf to paste the invitations."

"The she-wolf?"

"Alpha's girlfriend."

Alpha had a girlfriend. Since when did Alpha have a girlfriend? Hadn't he just been flirting with

Frankie three weeks ago? "I didn't know he had one," she said as coolly as she could.

"Oh, he's always got one. And she's always the she-wolf," said Matthew. "The girl may change; in fact, the girl will always change. But the name remains the same."

Hm. Frankie wondered if she had underestimated Alpha. When she'd met him at the rock wall, she had thought he either didn't remember her or was backing off because Matthew had claimed her. But now it seemed Alpha had already hooked up with the she-wolf, and if he always had someone, he was at least as popular with girls as Matthew. "Isn't he supposed to be an alpha *dog*?" Frankie asked. "Not a wolf?"

"Of course. But we're gentlemen. We'd never call a girl a—"

"I see. And Alpha got this she-wolf to make invitations?"

"They just started going out. She's still trying to impress him." Matthew laughed. "She hasn't realized yet that it's impossible."

Frankie absorbed the information. Who was the she-wolf? How had she managed to be already so in with this pack of boys that they'd had her make the invitations to their secret party?

And why was it impossible to impress Alpha?

Of course she couldn't ask Matthew any of these

questions, so she said something else. "You matched everyone up?"

He chuckled. "Yeah."

"So I'm guessing you wanted to take me to this party."

"Well," said Matthew, pushing her gently with his shoulder while keeping hold of her hand. "I wanted to take you *somewhere*. And I was geeking out and couldn't ask you to go get food or see a movie with me like a normal human."

"Right." Frankie was sarcastic.

"For real. So we got this idea to have a party, and I didn't have to ask you, but yet I still get to take you."

"Very slick."

"I manage incredible things while avoiding other things," said Matthew.

"Like what?"

"I organized a party so I wouldn't have to ask you out. I did two extra-credit response papers in English last year 'cause I was avoiding Italian vocabulary for the final. I built a boat this summer to keep from hanging around with a girl who—I don't know—thought she was my girlfriend. Or wanted to be, or something."

"You built a boat?"

"Just a putt-putt. At my family's place on the Vineyard. It's in a fishing village. Menemsha."

"I thought you—" Frankie thought Matthew had

driven cross-country with Dean and Alpha, but she cut herself short because she didn't want him to realize he'd been so important to her that she remembered his summer plans. And besides, he could have done both. "I thought you meant a sailboat."

"My uncle builds those, but no. This for putting around, maybe fishing, maybe going over to the Aquinnah side with my bike. Do you know the Vineyard?"

"No."

"Oh, I should show you around. There's this great biking area that you take a tiny ferry to—or a leaky putt-putt, if you're me. And guys are pulling lobsters right out of the sea and throwing them into a pot. You like lobster, don't you?"

Frankie thought: He'll show me around the Vineyard? What?

And then she thought: He likes me! He wants to see me in the summer. Which is months away.

And then she thought: How do I answer him?

Matthew let go of Frankie's hand and reached his arm around her shoulders, while her brain turned over his offer to show her around the Vineyard (it was several hours and a ferry ride away), his apparent ignorance that she was Jewish (and didn't eat shellfish), and his assumption that they would be hanging around together longer than just for tonight. Within 3.27

seconds she decided there was no direct response that wouldn't make her sound overeager, naive, self-conscious, or confused—although she was all four.

"Did you do any other matchups tonight?" she asked instead, thinking of Gidget and Callum.

"A few. Nothing too nefarious, though."

"Like what?"

"A buddy of mine we hooked up with a girl he likes. We put some friends together who don't know each other well. You know, seeing what would happen. We invited a few lowerclassmen, but not that many."

"So you didn't mastermind any conflicts, put people together with their archenemies, nothing like that?"

Matthew looked at her. "I'm not one for schadenfreude."

"What's that?"

"Happiness at the misfortunes of others."

Frankie liked that word. *Schadenfreude.* "I'm not either," she said. "But I might have been tempted anyway. To see what would happen to the social order if I made some unusual pairs."

"You have an evil little mind, do you know that?"

Frankie laughed.

"I'm serious. I bet you're trouble wrapped in a pretty package."

"Who says it's little?"

"What?"

"My evil mind. "

"Okay, a sizable evil mind. Wrapped in a pretty package. That was the point."

Frankie felt herself flush. "Thank you."

"You're welcome," said Matthew. "I like a girl who knows how to take a compliment. You know how so many girls are all, 'Oh, me? I'm not pretty. I'm a hag.'"

"Yeah."

"Well, it's so much nicer when someone just says thank you. So don't become that girl, okay?"

"That haggy girl? Okay."

They stepped out of the woods and headed up the path to the near edge of the golf course. "Frankie?"

"What?'

"That thing about me and Alpha organizing the party. You won't go telling your friends, or anything, will you?"

"No."

"Promise? Your lips are sealed?"

Frankie didn't see why it was such a big deal, but she nodded. "Don't worry," she told him. "I am exceptionally good at keeping secrets."

THE GOLF COURSE

THEY REACHED THE small clubhouse, with a garage for golf carts and storage lockers for students' clubs. The lights were off and the building was locked. For a moment, the night landscape seemed deserted. Frankie and Matthew skirted the side of the clubhouse and looked down the hill to the course.

Nearly forty people were walking down. All dressed in dark colors, many lugging beer and a few carrying blankets to spread out on the grass. Most were seniors, though Frankie could make out Star holding hands with Dean, who was easy to spot because he was wearing an orange hunting jacket.

Matthew grabbed her arm and they ran down the hill together.

* * *

An hour later, Frankie was cold, and so was everyone else. They had all underestimated what they'd needed to wear. The blankets people had brought to lie on ended up wrapped around the girls, and without blankets, there was nowhere to sit—so nearly everyone was standing.

People were drinking beer and smoking cigarettes, but there hadn't been that much beer (everyone was underage), and most of it was gone. Ash and cigarette butts littered the golf course, and Frankie felt irritated that no one was thinking to shove them into their beer bottles or even their pockets.

Matthew was flitting around. Playing host even though no one was supposed to know it was his party.

There was no one for Frankie to talk to. Most of the people there didn't know who she was. She stood alone, thinking. She knew she shouldn't be irritated that Matthew wasn't standing next to her—it was a party, and there were so many people here he'd probably barely talked to since last June. But as she looked at him laughing with Callum, Dean, and Alpha, Frankie remembered how Matthew had called her a "pretty package," how he'd called her mind little, how he'd told her not to change—as if he had some power over her. A tiny part of her wanted to go over to him and shout, "I can feel like a hag some days if I want! And I can tell everybody how insecure I am if I want! Or I can be pretty and pretend to think I'm a hag out of fake modesty—I can do that if I want, too. Because you, Livingston, are not the boss of me and what kind of girl I become."

But most of her simply felt happy that he had put his arm around her and told her he thought she was pretty.

Frankie sat down for a moment, but the grass was cold and slightly damp, so she stood again. She saw Porter—her ex, one of the only other sophomores there—talking to Callum on one edge of the group. She didn't want to see him, so she went the opposite direction and found Star. "You were right," Frankie said, tapping her on the shoulder. "I got an invitation."

Star turned. "Did I ask you about it?"

How could she not recall asking about the invitation? She must have known Matthew was interested in Frankie, because she had thought to ask Frankie about the party, rather than any of the more popular, more obvious underclassmen in their history class.

Frankie was trying to like Star, a feat she'd never before bothered to attempt. What with recent developments on the Matthew front, there seemed like a reasonable possibility she and Star would both be sophomore girlfriends of senior boys who were friends, so it was worthwhile getting to know one another. But Star's dismissal was annoying.

Frankie was beginning to realize that the kind of selective memory exhibited by Dean, Star, and their ilk was neither stupidity nor poor recollection. It was a power play—possibly subconscious on the part of the player—but nevertheless intended to discomfit another person who was in some way perceived as a threat. Maybe Star was threatened because Frankie was smart and Star was not; maybe because Star wanted to be the only sophomore girl with the high status of having a boyfriend in Matthew's set; or maybe because Star was generally insecure and suspicious of women and girls who weren't similar to her. In any case, she was threatened by Frankie, so she feigned forgetfulness, just as Dean had done.

"In history," Frankie reminded Star.

"That class is so boring." Star grimaced. "I can't stand it. Grigoryan starts talking and I go la-la-la up to my happy place in my head and wait for it to be over. You should see my notebook. It has some of the most complicated doodles in, like, the history of Alabaster."

"It's not so bad."

"Well, not compared to geometry," Star said.

"You didn't like that Napoleon lecture with the slides?"

"Um. No."

"With his short-man complex and his receding hairline and paunchy stomach? Didn't you kind of like that painting we saw this morning? And the whole thing about him being the Little Corporal, the one who knew all his soldiers' names?"

Star's friend Claudia came up. She was a tall redhead without a single freckle. A soccer player. Inclined to pepper her sentences with enormous words, the meanings of which were not entirely within her apprehension. "Hey-hey," she said to Star, with a nod at Frankie. "Look at this." She held up the envelope that had enclosed her blue invitation. "What kind of dog is that?" she said, pointing to the wax seal.

"I don't know," said Star. "Maybe a beagle?"

"Snoopy is a beagle," said Claudia with a shake of her head.

"But it looks kind of like Snoopy."

"Uh-uh. Snoopy's epicanthic folds aren't like that."

Star laughed. "Snoopy rules! He's the cutest dog."

"It's a basset hound," said Frankie.

"Snoopy's not a basset hound," said Claudia. "Snoopy's a beagle. I already told you."

"Yes, but—"

"Ooh, there's Dean," Star said to Frankie, pointing. "He's my boyfriend now, did you know that?"

Frankie nodded.

"I guess people talk. Anyway, I've gotta go remind

him how he's driving me off-campus to see a movie tomorrow. Come on, Claudia."

And they were off.

Frankie watched them go, ponytails swinging, and realized she had bored Star and Claudia so much that Star had made an excuse to get away.

But on the other hand, they had bored Frankie, too.

The party was boring. It was people standing around in the cold.

A little after one a.m., everyone started drifting into the woods, heading back to the dorms a few at a time so as not to make noise. Matthew walked Frankie home through the dark trees, holding her hand and whispering conspiratorially about wanting to be a newspaper editor and how last summer he, Dean, and Alpha had hitched a ride with the driver of a Mack truck when the Volvo had broken down, and had eaten pie at a truck stop for several hours before calling Triple-A.

He walked her to the woods behind her dorm. "Can I kiss you?" he whispered as she was opening her phone to call Trish.

How could he ask that?

How could he ever think she wouldn't?

"No way," she told him, and pulled him toward her.

"You're being mean to me," he whispered in her ear.

"Okay, I changed my mind," she said.

His lips were cold on the outside, and Frankie was shivering even with his arms around her.

Matthew stopped kissing her and breathed his warm breath down the back of her shirt, laughing. Then he kissed her again.

She didn't call Trish for another half hour.

Most young women, when confronted with the peculiarly male nature of certain social events—usually those incorporating beer or other substances guaranteed to kill off a few brain cells, and often involving either the freezing-cold outdoors or the near-suffocating heat of a filthy dorm room, but which can also, in more intellectual circles, include the watching of boring Russian films—will react in one of three ways.

Some, like Trish, will wonder what the point is, figure there probably is no point and never was one, and opt for typically feminine or domestic activities such as crumble-making, leaving whatever boyfriends they have to "hang with the guys."

Others, like Star, will be bored most of the time but will continue attending such events because they are the girlfriends or would-be girlfriends of said boys, and they don't want to seem like killjoys or harpies. If the boys are there, playing games on the Xbox (indoors) or letting off cherry bombs to make a big noise for no reason (outdoors), the girls will chatter among themselves and generally make a quiet display of being interested in whatever the boys think is interesting.

The third group aggressively embraces the activities at hand. These girls dislike the marginalized position such events naturally put them in, and they are determined not to stay on those margins. They do what the boys do wholeheartedly, if sometimes a little falsely. They drink beer, play video games, light off the cherry bombs. They remain alert during obscure Russian films. They even buy the beer, win the video games, and show up with an M-80, just when the cherry bombs are beginning to get old. If required by their social circle, they read articles on Andrei Tarkovsky.

Whether their enthusiasm is forced or entirely genuine, these girls gain respect from the boys—who are not, after all, cavemen, but enlightened twenty-first-century males who are happy to let females into their inner circles if the females prove their mettle.

As I said, most girls will engage in one of these three behaviors, but Frankie Landau-Banks did none. Although she went home that night feeling happier than she had ever been in her short life, she did not confuse the golf course party with a *good* party, and she did not tell herself that she had had a pleasant time.

It had been, she felt, a dumb event preceded by excellent invitations.

What Frankie did that was unusual was to imagine herself in control. The drinks, the clothes, the invitations, the instructions, the food (there had been none), the location, everything. She asked herself: If I were in charge, how could I have done it better?

A Garlic Knot

T HE NEXT DAY, Sunday, Frankie woke to the
sound of someone knocking. Trish was already
out, so Frankie went to the door in her pajamas. There stood Alpha, wearing a dark red sweater with
large holes in the elbows. He hadn't talked to her since
she'd met him in the gym. Even last night he'd done nothing more than nod at her as she stood next to Matthew on
the lawn. "Come down," he said now, as if it were the most
natural thing in the world. "We're going to get pizza."

What "we"?

She and Alpha?

Was he asking her out now? He must have known
she had gone to the party with Matthew.

Frankie stalled for time. "It's only ten o'clock," she
said.

"We'll call it brunch."

"Where are you getting pizza at this hour?"

"Luigi's in Lowell is open twenty-four hours."

"I'm not allowed off-campus," Frankie told him, still turning over in her mind whether she wanted to go. Only seniors could leave without express permission or supervision.

"Who's gonna know?" he asked her.

Alpha had a point. But such is the nature of the panopticon: most students at Alabaster didn't leave campus—even though it was as simple as hopping over a low stone wall. "I don't want to get caught," Frankie said, wondering if her pajama top was see-through and crossing her arms over her chest.

"Matthew went to pick up his car in the lot," Alpha told her. "He should be waiting for us at the gate in a couple minutes. He told me you'd be a sport."

Oh. Alpha was here for Matthew. It was okay.

She didn't have to choose.

"So. Are you gonna come get pizza?" Alpha asked. "Or are you gonna be a good little girl and stay on campus?"

"I'll be down in five," Frankie told him.

Matthew's car was a navy Mini Cooper. It was already running when Frankie and Alpha arrived at the gate.

"Shotgun," said Alpha.

Frankie felt a wave of annoyance, but it dissipated

on seeing Matthew's smile light up. "Hey there, Frankie. You ready for some serious pizza?"

She nodded and squeezed past Alpha's bulk into the backseat. Matthew put the car in gear.

"I would like to state at the outset," said Alpha, lighting a cigarette and rolling down his window, "that anything made outside Italy or the five boroughs of New York City has no legitimate claim to be called pizza."

"What should we call it?" asked Matthew.

"Call it a disk of dough with tomato and cheese. But it is not a pizza."

"A DOD," said Matthew.

"If you must." Alpha exhaled. "We'll go have a rubbery, bready DOD. And it will be better than the food in the caf, and it will be nice to have a big pile of grease and salt first thing on a Sunday morning, but it won't be pizza."

"You are such a snob, dog."

"I am not. Pizza is a food of the people. It's cheap, you can get it on any street corner in the city. It's categorically impossible to be snobby about pizza."

"Do you remember that Russian diner we stopped at in Chicago where that lady with the hair growing out of her nose wouldn't let you put ketchup on your steak?" asked Matthew.

"Yeah, so?"

"So it's possible to be snobby about anything. That wasn't even a good steak," said Matthew. "And she was not going to let you put ketchup on it even if it killed her."

"What's your feeling about pineapple?" asked Frankie from the back.

"On a pizza?" said Alpha. "Unforgivable."

"How come?"

"Because it's fruit. There's no fruit on a pizza."

"A tomato's a fruit."

"That doesn't count." Alpha took a drag of his smoke. "A tomato may be a fruit, but it is a singular fruit. A savory fruit. A fruit that has ambitions far beyond the ambitions of other fruits."

"Really."

"Sure. It's a staple ingredient in Italian cooking. You put it in sauces, you put it in salad with a little mozzarella and olive oil, you make ratatouille. And what do you do with your average fruit? Nothing. You just eat it. No one is going to found a whole cuisine on a grape."

"What about wine?" asked Frankie.

"Okay, okay. But grapefruit? No. Or pineapple? No. Can you imagine founding a cuisine on blueberries? Everyone would be so sick of them within a week, they'd starve to death. The blueberry has no versatility. The country with a cuisine based on the blueberry would be a country of lunatics, turned mad by the unwavering sameness of their daily meals."

"Okay," said Frankie. "But have you actually tried pineapple pizza?"

"I don't have to try it," said Alpha. "It's disgusting."

"How can you write it off when you haven't tried it?"

"She caught you, dog," laughed Matthew. "Pizza snobbery is coming out of your pores right now."

"Oh, bull." Alpha threw his cigarette butt out the window and pouted.

"You're not a pie snob, I'll say that," said Matthew, consoling him. "Frankie, we drove across the country this summer for three weeks trying to eat as many different kinds of pie as we could—"

"I—"

"What?"

Frankie had been going to say, "I know," but had thought better of it. "Nothing."

"Anyway," continued Matthew, "Alpha was a completely egalitarian pie lover. He liked everything. Whereas by like, day three, Dean had narrowed it down to only one kind he liked enough to be eating every day."

"Which was?"

"Lemon meringue. But then he'd only eat half of it anyway."

"That was abnormal," said Alpha. "I mean, I ask you: is it normal to eat only half a piece of pie?"

"I don't think so," said Frankie. "If it's in front of me, I want it."

"What about ice cream?" asked Alpha. "Or frozen custard?"

Frankie was speechless for a moment.

Alpha did remember her.

That day on the beach.

She had figured he did. Probably.

But it was good to be sure.

Though now, it wasn't something they could talk about. Because she was with Matthew.

She had picked Matthew. Or he had picked her.

Or Alpha had picked the she-wolf. Or something.

"I've eaten half a frozen custard before," Frankie told him. "But custard has a cold factor. It's never too cold or too warm for pie."

"It's never too cold for custard, either," said Alpha. "Not in my universe." He reached into the glove box and shuffled through the CDs. "If you don't like food, you don't like sex," he continued. "I bet that's Dean's problem. His grades are so excellent because he's completely repressed."

"I doubt that," said Matthew.

"Why do you think he's going out with that ball of fluff half his age? Sorry, Frankie."

"Star's all right." Matthew turned off the highway.

"You don't like Star?" Frankie asked. She'd seen Star sitting at the senior tables more than once, talking and laughing with Dean's friends.

"Oh wait, she's not a ball of fluff, she's a DOD," said Alpha. "Like she's fine, she's okay, but she's not— delicious. Which is perfect for Dean, because he's so repressed anyway, he's not interested in delicious."

"That has nothing to do with her being a sopho-more," Frankie argued.

But she was out of her depth.

They pulled into Luigi's, which turned out to be a dark place with red Formica tables and a pinball machine in the back, catering to the late-night crowd from the bar next door. NO PIZZA TILL NOON, read a sign on the counter.

"Is there really no pizza?" Matthew asked a bus-boy.

"The guy who makes it didn't come in," was the answer. "Sunday morning, nobody wants to get up and make pizza. We got soda. We got garlic knots."

"I'll take garlic knots," said Alpha. "Let's get, I don't know, what? A dozen of them to go."

There was a Ms. Pac-Man machine in the back of the restaurant. Frankie felt in her bag for some quar-ters and fed them in. While her little Pac-lady chomped energy pellets, she listened to the boys talk. They were sitting in a booth near the front.

"Those are like the ultimate DODs," said Matthew. "All dough, no tomato, no cheese."

"No, they're BODS," said Alpha. "Balls of dough. But"—he sniffed the bag—"these have got a serious garlic punch, I'd say. We shouldn't underestimate them."

"Lemme smell." Matthew stuck his face in the bag.

"What do you want to bet your new girl doesn't eat them?" Alpha said to Matthew under his breath.

"I don't want to bet," said Matthew, taking one out of the bag and popping it into his mouth. "I never bet on what girls will eat."

"That's the thing about women," said Alpha, drumming his fingers on the Formica tabletop. "They're not voracious."

"You don't think?"

Alpha ate another garlic knot. "Maybe they are, somewhere inside. But they don't act on it. They're always eating half the custard and then giving the rest of the cone away."

There it was again. The custard. Alpha wanted Frankie to know he remembered. And that, somehow, he was disappointed in her.

Was that why he hadn't pursued her? Because he could have, couldn't he? Despite Matthew's interest?

He thought she wasn't voracious. That she didn't go after what she wanted. That she was a girl who left the boardwalk as soon as her mother called her cell.

"That makes Dean a woman," said Matthew. "He left half-eaten pie all across the country."

Alpha laughed. "He is a woman. About some things."

Frankie didn't like garlic. It made her nauseated. But she forced Ms. Pac-Man to eat the last of the pellets in her video maze and left the intermission between levels to play on its own while she walked to the booth where Matthew and Alpha were sitting.

"Weren't you getting those to go?" she asked, sitting down and pointing at the bag of garlic knots.

"Yeah, but where are we going?" asked Alpha. "They'll stink up the Mini Cooper anyway."

"Let me have one," she told him.

He handed her the open bag.

Wincing only slightly, she ate the knot in two bites.

"Last night he said he wanted to show me around the Vineyard," Frankie gushed, on the phone with Zada later that afternoon.

"Typical," Zada said. "That's a classic Matthew move."

Earlier, Frankie had kissed Matthew good-bye in a haze of garlic fumes before he ran off to soccer practice.

Then the sky had cracked open and it began to rain. Now she was walking through campus on her way to the library, holding an umbrella and stepping deliberately in rain puddles. She was wearing red rubber boots.

"What's typical?" Frankie asked her sister.

"I'm not saying he's a bad guy or anything. I like Matthew," answered Zada. "I've just noticed that's how he operates. Once he decides he likes someone, he's like insanely welcoming."

"So you're saying it's not just to me."

"No, it's not. But it *is* only to people he really likes. I think it's a coping strategy to dissipate anxiety about his wealth and his family. Do you know what I mean?"

"Not exactly." Frankie didn't want to hear Zada's interpretation of the Livingston psychology. She just wanted to be happy Matthew liked her and wanted to take her to his summerhouse.

"It's like this," explained Zada. "Matthew knows some people will back off from being friends with him because of his dad's position in the world. Like they won't invite him places or ask him to do stuff because they assume he's always got somewhere better to be. Or 'cause they don't think they belong in his exalted circles." Zada paused. "Hold on. I'm in the coffeehouse and I just have to order. Can I get a carrot-walnut muffin, a fruit salad, and a soy latte?"

Frankie had reached the library and was standing outside under her umbrella, waiting for Zada to finish.

"Okay. Frankie. I'm back. What was I saying?"

"About Matthew."

"Oh, yeah. Elizabeth Heywood told me that his Vineyard house had like six people sleeping in the guest rooms last summer. Matthew had invited Elizabeth when he barely knew her—just like a spur of the moment thing when they'd run into each other in a bookstore in Boston. When she went out there, there were all these people sleeping over. It's a huge, huge house, and some of them were just random people Matthew had met that summer, guys who were waiting tables on summer break. His parents were living in the guesthouse."

"That's weird."

"You want to hear my analysis?" asked Zada.

"I can't stop you anyway."

"Okay. Playing host—or promising to—is like how Matthew dispels anxieties people have about his social position. And—this is where it gets complicated—it paradoxically lets him solidify that exalted position."

"What?"

"Because he's letting people see the day-to-day workings of his super-privileged life. It lets him be the host, the most important one in the room."

"Uh-huh."

"What do you think?" Zada always wanted Frankie to agree with her insights.

"I think you're reading too much sociology or whatever."

"Never too much," said Zada. "I gotta go now. But think about it."

She clicked off.

A TRIANGLE

THE SHE-WOLF TURNED out to be Elizabeth Heywood, the girl who'd been to Matthew's Vineyard house. Frankie knew Elizabeth slightly through Zada. She wasn't part of Alpha's crowd, really—but she was still a strong match for Alpha in that she had spent her late-elementary and middle-school years as a featured actor on a popular sitcom, playing the cynical daughter of a famous comedian. She had started Alabaster as a freshman the year the show ended, but it was still in regular syndication. Part of any new freshman's orientation the past three years was seeing Elizabeth across the dining room, looking older and a bit prettier than her on-screen character.

Frankie knew that Elizabeth had earned the

money that was putting her through Alabaster. She had also earned the money that paid for her red Mercedes, which she described as "payback for having spent my childhood working with a bunch of coke addicts and manipulative harpies"—so she differed from her fellow students in the way that new money differs from old.

She was extremely well known around campus—without being exactly popular. She was more of a floater, comfortable in a number of different social clusters but firmly ensconced in none. She had the wide, freckled face and big dimples you see so often in child actors who've been picked to look particularly all-American, and her hair, which had been dyed red on television, was brown. Her speech was spacey and slightly slurred, a trait that had made her Q-rating extremely high in the days of her show's greatest popularity.

Elizabeth and Alpha were rarely seen together unless as part of a group, and they were completely unaffectionate. Although they'd been going out only a few weeks, they bickered at each other like old marrieds.

When you go to boarding school, and the usual obstacles of transportation and suspicious parents are removed from the equation, relationships can progress quickly. This truism applied not only to Alpha and

Elizabeth, but also to Frankie and Matthew. Matthew was warm and publicly affectionate. In less than a week from the night of the golf course party, Frankie was a regular at his table in the caf.

The table was always Matthew, Alpha, Dean, and Callum—and (more often than anyone particularly wanted her) Star. Most of the time they were joined by Elizabeth, Tristan, and Steve (both lacrosse players and relatively unimportant to this chronicle). The guys threw bread rolls and argued politics. They gossiped and talked sports and leaned so far back in their chairs it seemed certain that they would capsize—although they never did. They had more fun than anyone else in the room.

Frankie was very happy.

Her favorite quality of Matthew's was his seeming immunity to embarrassment. For example, Alpha said something at dinner so ridiculous that Matthew snorted juice out his nose and down the front of his shirt. Anyone else Frankie knew would have blushed and stammered his way out of the caf as quickly as possible, changing his shirt immediately and praying never to speak of the apple juice snort ever again.

But Matthew stood, raised his arms in victory, and proclaimed himself the grodiest human being in all of Alabaster, daring anyone to challenge him. "Come hither, come all. Rise to the challenge. See if you can top the Livingston Apple Juice Snort! We seriously doubt this supreme level of grodieness can be surpassed, but we invite you all to attempt it, and support you in your endeavors."

Dean tried making a pink mountain of ketchup and mashed potato, then licking it with his quite disgustingly long tongue—but was voted no match for the LAJS. Alpha made a farty noise with his armpit, but he too, was nowhere near grodie enough. "Public decency prevents me from being a true contender," he said. "I do not concede defeat. I am too much of a good citizen to perform acts of serious grodieness while innocent underclassmen are attempting to eat their mystery meat."

Callum claimed he had no such inhibitions and proceeded to drop all his croutons into his orange juice and drain the glass.

"That isn't so much grodieness as self-punishment," argued Matthew. "The person you're grossing out is yourself. And you have to admit, that's a remarkably poor strategy."

Callum conceded defeat, and they stood to clear their trays. Matthew put one hand low on Frankie's back. She wouldn't have thought she could feel attracted to a boy who had just sprayed apple juice out his nose, but she was.

Later, however, she couldn't help but notice that of the five people at the table (including Matthew), she was the only one whom no one had expected to do anything disgusting.

Nor had she volunteered.

As the weeks passed, Frankie began to see that although Matthew welcomed people into his world with surprising warmth—it didn't occur to him to enter anyone else's. She had to introduce him to Trish three times before he recognized her on his own, and he almost never came to Frankie's dorm room. If he wanted her, he called and asked her to come out and meet him.

He didn't know any of Frankie's Debate Club friends or the sophomores she hung out with from classes. He wasn't curious about her family. He expected her to become part of his life, but he didn't become part of hers.

Lots of girls don't notice when they are in this situation. They are so focused on their boyfriends that they don't remember they had a life at all before their romances, so they don't become upset that the boyfriend isn't interested.

Frankie did notice—but she wasn't sure she cared. She had never felt a wild connection to the kids she was friendly with from freshman year. She was very fond of Trish, but Trish was wrapped up in Artie. And Frankie not only adored Matthew—she adored his world. He and his friends seemed . . . better than her and hers.

Not because of money.

Not because of popularity.

Expensive clothes and high status had little effect on Frankie. But their money and popularity made life extremely easy for Matthew, Dean, Alpha, and Callum. They did not need to impress anyone and were therefore remarkably free from snarkiness, anxiety, and irksome aspirational behaviors, such as competition over grades and evaluation of one another's clothing. They were not afraid to break the rules, because consequences rarely applied to them. They were free. They were silly. They were secure.

Frankie and Matthew had been going out for two weeks when he first blew her off for Alpha. They were walking together after dinner, strolling down to the pond just to be somewhere pretty—the way people do when they are first going out—when Matthew's cell rang.

Instead of switching it off, as he had the first two weeks of their coupledom, Matthew flipped it open. "Hey, dog," he said, then listened for a few minutes. Frankie could hear Alpha's raspy tenor from the phone. "I gotta go," Matthew said, hanging up and kissing Frankie on the cheek three times to show he was still crazy for her. "There's a study session for calc. I spaced."

And he was gone.

She stood beside the pond at dusk, all by herself.

The second time and the third were the same. Alpha called and made some demand—and Matthew disappeared. Each time it was something Frankie could neither fight nor ask to attend: a senior study session, a newspaper meeting, fund-raising for the soccer team. But it was always Alpha who called, and Frankie wasn't dumb.

He was marking his territory.

Matthew.

Even more often, however, Alpha and the boys came to Matthew—so much so that it occasionally seemed to Frankie as if she were dating all of them at once. She and Matthew would be studying in the library or walking toward the caf for dinner, and the dogs would run up around them, laughing and jostling each other, loud and merry. Tristan would grab Frankie and swing her around (he was a big guy, rowing last on the heavy eight), while Callum would quiz her about girls he found attractive in the sophomore class. Or Alpha would insert himself between her and Matthew, reaching an arm around each of them as they walked, and she would be disconcerted by the heavy weight of his hand on her waist. Whatever she and

Matthew had been discussing would fall away in favor of whatever Alpha wanted to talk about.

Once, Matthew, Alpha, and Steve—on their way back from a soccer game—spotted Frankie on her way to meet Trish at the pool. They followed her and insisted on getting in the pool in their uniform shorts, all of them pushing each other in the diving section and doing cannonballs off the board.

Trish kicked back and forth with Frankie for twenty minutes and then excused herself to take a shower. But Frankie heaved herself out of the lap pool and dove into the deep end with the boys.

She didn't mind them being there. Not then; not ever, really.

Yes, she wanted to be alone with Matthew, but she loved the way the world lit up when the boys were around—loved how they bantered with one another, teased each other, talked with one another urgently. Like the best kind of family.

Often, Matthew would take her hand when they appeared. Or touch her foot under the table, so she knew he was still thinking of her. And the dogs would mix juice and soda together, or quiz each other on dates for history, or draw ridiculous doodles in their notebooks, or make ornate paper airplanes instead of studying—and Frankie would be a part of it. Almost.

The Neglected Positive

OW DOES A PERSON become the person she is? What are the factors in her culture, her childhood, her education, her religion, her economic stature, her sexual orientation, her race, her everyday interactions—what stimuli lead her to make choices other people will despise her for?

This chronicle is an attempt to mark out the contributing elements in Frankie Landau-Banks's character. What led her to do what she did: things she would later view with a curious mixture of hubris and regret. Frankie's mental processes had been stimulated by Ms. Jensson's lectures on the panopticon, her encounters with Alpha, her mother's refusal to let her walk into town at the Jersey Shore, her observation of the joy Matthew took in rescuing her from her bicycle accident, and her anger at Dean for not remembering her. All these were factors in what happened next. And here is another:

You will remember that Frankie was reading P. G. Wodehouse's *The Code of the Woosters*, for fun. She had left it on the floor of the library the night she got the golf-course party invitation from Matthew, but the next day she went back and borrowed it. The book must not be discounted as an influence on her behavior, for a number of reasons.

First, the young men in that and in many of Wodehouse's other novels—several of which Frankie also read—are members of the Drones club. The Drones is a British gentlemen's club populated by silly young blots with pockets full of money and too much free time. Unlike any of the other clubs described in this chronicle, the Drones has a permanent location. There is a swimming pool, a restaurant, and numerous lounges for smoking, drinking, and trading stories. Bertie Wooster, Gussie Fink-Nottle, Catsmeat Potter-Pirbright, and all Wodehouse's other characters forged their bonds at boarding school. They base many of their ethical and financial decisions (Shall I recommend him a bet? Lend him money? Ask him a favor?) upon whether a fellow is an old school chum—or not.

The Drones are always up for fun. They steal policemen's helmets, wager heavily on school sack races, trick one another into falling, fully-clothed, into swimming pools. And while they're mostly too dim-witted to be future members of Parliament or editors of newspapers—and many of them are intermittently broke—they are well and firmly Old Boys.

Second, Mr. Wodehouse is a prose stylist of such startling talent that Frankie nearly skipped around with glee when she first read some of his phrases. Until her discovery of *Something Fresh* on the top shelf of Ruth's bookshelf one bored summer morning, Frankie's leisure reading had consisted primarily of paperback mysteries she found on the spinning racks at the public library down the block from her house, and the short stories of Dorothy Parker. Wodehouse's jubilant word-play bore itself into her synapses like a worm into a fresh ear of corn.

"He spoke with a certain what-is-it in his voice, and I could see that, if not actually being disgruntled, he was far from being gruntled."
        —*The Code of the Woosters*

Frankie read this line, one that Wodehouse fans love and repeat over and over to one another (though she didn't know that then), and her mind began to whir.

"Come kiss me," she said to Matthew. They were

in the library common room on a Sunday afternoon, studying. Frankie had finished what work she planned to do, and was reading Wodehouse to keep Matthew company.

He got up from the desk, walked over to the couch on which she sat, and kissed her on the lips. There was no one else around.

"Mmmm," she whispered. "Now I'm gruntled."

"What?"

"Gruntled. I was disgruntled before."

"Why?"

"It's drizzling, there's nothing to do but study, the vending machine's broken. You know, disgruntled."

"And now, you're . . ."

"Gruntled."

She had expected Matthew's face to light at the new word, but he touched her chin lightly and said, "I don't think that word means what you think it means."

"What?" Frankie didn't think it was a word. She thought it was—she thought it was what she'd later call a "neglected positive."

Prefixes like "in," "non," "un," "dis," and "im" make words negative, yes? There may be grammatical particulars I am not addressing here, but generally speaking. So you have a positive word like "restrained," and you add the prefix "un" to get a negative: *unrestrained*.

Possible. *Impossible.*

Sane. *Insane.*

When there's a negative word or expression—*immaculate*, for example—but the positive is almost never used, and you choose to use it, you become rather amusing. Or pretentious. Or pretentiously amusing, which can sometimes be good. In any case, you are uncovering a buried word. The neglected positive of *immaculate* is *maculate*, meaning morally blemished or stained. The neglected positive of *insufferable* is *sufferable*—meaning bearable—though no one ever uses it.

Other times, the neglected positive is *not* a word. It is then an imaginary neglected positive, or INP (inpea).

(Frankie made up everything that follows after the stuff about *maculate* and *sufferable*, just in case you thought of impressing your English teacher with your knowledge of the inpea.)

Some inpeas: *Impetuous* means hotheaded, unthinking, impulsive. The positive of it doesn't exist, so you can make a new, illegitimate word.

Petuous, meaning careful.

Ept, meaning competent, from *inept*.

Turbed, meaning relaxed and comfortable, from *disturbed*.

You can make more inpeas by pretending that something is a negative when it's not a negative—because, you justify, it has one of those prefixy-sounding things at the beginning.

Impugn—it means to call into question, to attack with words. It comes from Latin *in-* (against) plus *pugnare* (to fight). *Pugn* by itself—although there is no such word—should technically mean to fight, like to fistfight. But to the ardent neglected positivist, *to pugn* would be to speak well of something.

Yet another technique of the neglected positivist is to impose a new meaning on a word that exists but, through the convolutions of grammar, doesn't technically mean what you are deciding it means. The neglected positive of *incriminate* is *criminate*, which actually, technically means the same thing as incriminate—because the *in-* isn't really making a negative in this case—but it is much more amusing if you use it to mean the opposite. *Criminate*: to give someone an alibi.

When you redefine a word like this, you are making a false neglected positive, as opposed to an imaginary neglected positive, and it can be useful to term these falsies FNPs or finnips. But *falsie* is more entertaining, so Frankie went with that. Later, when she thought all this through.

Gruntled is a falsie, though Frankie didn't know it until Matthew explained it to her (though not in those terms, of course).

"*Gruntled* means grumpy," he said, walking over

to the dictionary, which stood on a large stand. He flipped some pages. "It doesn't mean happy, it means . . . look, *to gruntle* is to grunt repeatedly, like to complain, or even better, to grumble." Flipping to the D section—"*Disgruntled* comes from the same middle-English source."

"Why?" Frankie was cross that he was being so literal. "That makes no sense, because if gruntled means grumbly, then disgruntled should mean un-grumbly."

"Umm . . ." Matthew scanned the dictionary. "*Dis*-can be an intensifier, as well as a negative."

Frankie bounced on the couch. "I like my version better."

Matthew took the dictionary off the stand and hiked himself up to sit on the small table. "My dad works in the newspaper business," he said. "I don't know if I told you that yet."

As if everyone at school didn't already know who his dad was.

"He started as a copy editor, and he used to make us play dictionary games at our summerhouse. So I learned, on fear of public humiliation, to look up any word I wasn't absolutely sure about."

Frankie didn't want Matthew to be right. In fact, a later Internet search proved that *gruntled* can indeed mean happy, but it's a back-formation from *disgruntled* that probably started with *The Code of the Woosters*, so today it legitimately means both one thing, and its opposite.

But by the time Frankie found *that* out, she was way beyond sharing it with Matthew.

What annoyed her now was not that Matthew was right—but that he wouldn't just enjoy the made-up word. That he *needed* to be right. And that he'd chucked her—actually chucked her under the chin, like you do to a dog, when informing her that, essentially, her cleverness with *gruntled* had been completely trumped by his stellar memory for obscure bits of the dictionary.

"It was a joke," she told him.

"I know," he said. "But it's only funny if you're really making up a word, and in this case you're not."

"You don't have to make me feel like such a nimrod."

"I was only pointing out what I thought you'd want to know."

"Way to take the fun out of it."

"Don't be so sensitive, Frankie."

"I'm not."

"You're pouting over a word in the dictionary."

"Fine." Frankie went back to her book, but she didn't read. If she was too sensitive, she thought, she was never going to last with this boy, this marvelous boy who made her feel dizzy when he kissed her.

She'd lose this world she'd gotten into, the brash rhythms of traded insults, the unembarrassed self-immolation, the giddy ridiculousness of Matthew and his friends. She could see immediately that being shrill or needy was the fastest way to lose her place among them.

She was not only worried about losing her boyfriend's affection. She was worried about losing her status with his friends.

Matthew had made Frankie feel *delible*. Yes, that was a good word for it.

She pulled out a sheet of notebook paper and began to make a list.

Cheese Fries

A FEW E-MAILS SENT in early October, which were later to fall into hands other than those of the intended recipients:

From: Porter Welsch [pw034@alabasterpreparatory.edu]
To: Frances Landau-Banks [fl202@alabasterpreparatory.edu]
Subject: Hey

Frankie, what's up? Hope your term is going well so far. I want to apologize for what happened with Bess last year.
—Porter

> **From:** Frances Landau-Banks
>   [fl202@alabasterpreparatory.edu]
> **To:** Porter Welsch [pw034@alabasterpreparatory.edu]
> **Subject:** Re: Hey
>
> You mean, you *want* to apologize, or you *are* apologizing? Your grammar is indistinct.

From: Porter Welsch [pw034@alabasterpreparatory.edu]
To: Frances Landau-Banks [fl202@alabasterpreparatory.edu]
Subject: This is me, apologizing

I apologize.

> **From:** Frances Landau-Banks
>   [fl202@alabasterpreparatory.edu]
> **To:** Porter Welsch [pw034@alabasterpreparatory.edu]
> **Subject:** Advertent Vaguery
>
> Also, "for what happened with Bess." Meaning, what?
> Is your vaguery advertent?

From: Porter Welsch [pw034@alabasterpreparatory.edu]
To: Frances Landau-Banks [fl202@alabasterpreparatory.edu]
Subject: Re: Advertent Vaguery—NOT

Vaguery was inadvertent.
For fooling around with Bess behind your back.
You let nothing slide, do you?

> **From:** Frances Landau-Banks
>   [fl202@alabasterpreparatory.edu]
> **To:** Porter Welsch [pw034@alabasterpreparatory.edu]
> **Subject:** Re: Re: Advertent Vaguery—NOT
>
> Nothing. But why apologize now? Why not over the
> summer, or at the start of school?

From: Porter Welsch [pw034@alabasterpreparatory.edu]
To: Frances Landau-Banks [fl202@alabasterpreparatory.edu]
Subject: Burger

Now, because I am feeling apologetic.
How about a burger on Wednesday at the Front Porch?

From: Frances Landau-Banks
     [fl202@alabasterpreparatory.edu]
To: Porter Welsch [pw034@alabasterpreparatory.edu]
Subject: Re: Burger

Why should I have a burger with you? Give me three reasons.

From: Porter Welsch [pw034@alabasterpreparatory.edu]
To: Frances Landau-Banks [fl202@alabasterpreparatory.edu]
Subject: Why Burger?

Free burger bought by me.
Because I would like to be friends.
Because there's something I want to talk to you about.

From: Frances Landau-Banks
     [fl202@alabasterpreparatory.edu]
To: Porter Welsch [pw034@alabasterpreparatory.edu]
Subject: Wednesday Burger

I always get fries, no burger. I am a vegetarian. You should remember that about me.

From: Porter Welsch [pw034@alabasterpreparatory.edu]
To: Frances Landau-Banks [fl202@alabasterpreparatory.edu]
Subject: Re: Wednesday Burger

You always get CHEESE fries. See? Am not a complete nimrod.

From: Frances Landau-Banks
     [fl202@alabasterpreparatory.edu]
To: Porter Welsch [pw034@alabasterpreparatory.edu]
Subject: Nimrod

What do you want to talk about?

From: Porter Welsch [pw034@alabasterpreparatory.edu]
To: Frances Landau-Banks [fl202@alabasterpreparatory.edu]
Subject: Re: Nimrod

I'll tell you when I see you.
xo Porter

> **From:** Frances Landau-Banks
>   [fl202@alabasterpreparatory.edu]
> **To:** Porter Welsch [pw034@alabasterpreparatory.edu]
> **Subject:** XO
>
> Don't xo me, Porter. Just because I'm letting you buy me
> cheese fries doesn't mean you can xo me.

From: Porter Welsch [pw034@alabasterpreparatory.edu]
To: Frances Landau-Banks [fl202@alabasterpreparatory.edu]
Subject: Re: XO

o, then.
P

> **From:** Frances Landau-Banks
>   [fl202@alabasterpreparatory.edu]
> **To:** Porter Welsch [pw034@alabasterpreparatory.edu]
> **Subject:** O
>
> Do you *want* to irritate me?

From: Porter Welsch [pw034@alabasterpreparatory.edu]
To: Frances Landau-Banks [fl202@alabasterpreparatory.edu]
Subject: Re: O

OOOOOOOOOOOOOOOOOOOOOOOO

"Why does he want to go to the Front Porch?" Frankie
complained to Trish late Saturday night. They were

sitting on their twin beds in the dorm, wearing pajamas. Frankie was supposedly studying for a history test, and Trish was thumbing through *Chicken Soup for the Horse Lover's Soul*. "I already accepted his apology. Now he's sending me hug e-mails and trying to buy me cheese fries; it seems unnecessary."

"He wants to be friends," said Trish. "He can only feel good about himself and what he did with Bess if you let him send you hug e-mails."

"Do you think I have to tell Matthew I'm going to lunch?"

"Yes."

"Why?"

"Would you want Matthew going to lunch with one of his exes?"

"No."

"Behind your back?"

"More no."

"So you have to tell him," concluded Trish. "It's mature."

Frankie's cell was charging on the nightstand. She called Matthew. "I have to go out for food with my ex-boyfriend," she told him. "On Wednesday."

"That one who cheated on you with Bess?"

"I've only had one boyfriend before."

"Besides me."

"Besides you." She felt warm inside, hearing him

call himself her boyfriend. "He wants to buy me cheese fries to make himself feel better."

"Aw, don't go."·

"No, I gotta go."

"Why? You don't owe that guy anything. Did he ever apologize to you, by the way?"

"Yes, actually he did."

"So what else is there to say? Stand him up. Come with me and we'll have a picnic down by the pond instead."

It would have been so easy just to say yes and to avoid the argument that seemed to be brewing. Part of Frankie wanted to say yes. But she was seriously curious what Porter had to say, and she'd already promised to go. "It's only cheese fries at the Front Porch," she told Matthew.

"I know, but you're letting him walk all over you."

Frankie stood and began pacing the floor. "No I'm not. He just wants to talk to me."

Trish interrupted. "Is Matthew being jealous?"

Frankie waved at her to shush, as Matthew said: "Yeah, but he doesn't deserve to talk to you."

"Nothing's gonna happen," Frankie said into the phone.

"I just don't think you should go. Don't let him push you around."

Since when was anyone pushing her around? That was just insulting.

"What's he saying?" whispered Trish.

"I don't let guys walk all over me," said Frankie to Matthew. "Just because Porter *did*, doesn't mean I *let* him."

"Okay."

She hated the offended tenor that had just shot through his voice. But she said what she felt anyway: "Please don't tell me what to do."

"What?"

"Don't tell me what to do."

Matthew sounded genuinely surprised. "I would never tell you what to do."

"You just told me not to go to lunch with Porter!"

"But you said you didn't want to go. I was encouraging you to stand up for yourself."

"I never said I didn't want to go!" Frankie cried in frustration.

She could hear Matthew's door slam and Alpha's voice say "Hey, dog, what's taking you so long?"

Matthew's voice suddenly turned sunny. "Alpha's here. Frankie, I'm gonna have to go."

"Fine."

"Don't be mad, 'kay?"

"Maybe." How could he just hang up in the middle of the argument?

"Go do whatever you want. Whatever you want, 'kay?"

"Okay."

"Don't be mad."

"All right. All right."

"You're not mad? Don't be mad, because I'm crazy about you."

"I'm not mad." And she wasn't. Not exactly. He sounded so plaintive, so warm—wondering if she were mad.

"Good," Matthew said. "I gotta go, Alpha needs to talk to me. Good night, baby."

"Good night."

Frankie flipped the phone closed. "He's letting me go," she told Trish.

"Letting you? Since when does he let you?" Trish sat up in bed.

"No, it wasn't like that. It's not that he's *letting* me. He just didn't want me to."

"So he was jealous."

"Maybe. But he doesn't want me to be mad about it. And he ended up saying I could do whatever I wanted."

"How did you go from *you* telling *him* not to push you around to him letting you go?" asked Trish. "That's a big leap."

"Yeah." Frankie flipped her pillow over and switched out the light. "I'm not sure how that happened."

123

THE T-SHIRT

○

HE NEXT DAY, Matthew gave Frankie his Superman T-shirt. This was a royal blue, paper-thin T-shirt he'd had for three years. She had noticed him in it many times her freshman year, his heavy shoulders, narrow waist, and black-rimmed glasses giving him much the look of Clark Kent—a superhero body underneath journalist drag. So when Matthew wore that shirt, it was like he was still Clark Kent, only Clark Kent wearing the Superman insignia, which was very meta. And hot.

Matthew never took off his glasses unless he was kissing her. When she saw him without them, he didn't look like Superman at all. He looked confused, like something was missing. She'd looked through the glasses once and realized he was massively nearsighted.

The afternoon Frankie got the T-shirt was one of the few times they really managed to be alone in the dorm room Matthew shared with Dean. It was Sunday afternoon, and most of their friends had taken the school vans into town, where they would eat lunch, prowl shops, and hide from the junior-level teachers who accompanied them. Normally, girls were only allowed in the boys' dorms from seven until nine thirty at night, "co-study hours," for which they formally had to sign in. So that day Matthew snuck Frankie into his third-floor room via the fire escape, which could be reached by climbing a tree adjacent to a hedge, which connected to the ladder, upon which you climbed to the third floor, entered through the bathroom, and went down the hall.

They listened to music and made out on Matthew's bed for a while. Then they played Scrabble and downloaded some music. At one point, Frankie noticed a droopy-eyed figurine of a basset hound on Matthew's bedside table—the kind you see in Hallmark shops or in your great-grandmother's parlor room, covered with a light film of dust. The paint was worn off on the nose, and the paws were chipped. "Who's your friend?" Frankie asked, putting it together immediately that Matthew's dog was the dog on the invitation, which was the dog of Senior's secret society.

"Please don't touch that."

"Why?" Frankie set the dog down and stroked its china ears. "Is it valuable?"

"I doubt it."

"Well then, why?" She hoped he would tell her, share his secrets with her.

"Just sentimental value. Could you, um, stop touching it, like I asked?"

Frankie took her hand off the basset and looked at Matthew. "I'm not going to break it. What's the deal?"

Matthew reached out and grabbed her hand, smiling. "I am not going to tell you. Come back here on the bed with me."

She stayed where she was. "I don't see what the big secret is," she pouted—although she did.

"It's not a big secret, I just don't want to discuss it."

"Fine."

"Frankie."

"What?"

"Please don't have hurt feelings."

"I don't."

"You are my girlfriend," whispered Matthew. "You're my girl and I'm your guy, and you're my girl and I'm your guy. Let's not fight."

"But I can't touch your china doggie."

"No," he said, kissing her. "You can't touch my china doggie."

* * *

They made out some more, and then it was getting late so Frankie stood and bent to get her sweater off the floor. Matthew, perhaps feeling bad that he hadn't let her touch his basset hound, grabbed the Superman shirt out of his drawer and handed it to her. "Here," he told her. "Put this on."

She had to take her shirt off to put it on, and for a moment she hesitated.

He was more experienced than she was, obviously. He was looking at her like taking her shirt off would be nothing. "Turn around," she told him.

"What?"

"Turn around, I'm not changing my clothes in front of you."

He flopped obligingly onto the bed, facedown into a pillow. "Mrwwfflfe," he said into the down.

"What?"

"Sometimes I forget you're only fifteen," he said.

Frankie was half touched and half hurt, but she put the T-shirt on. It smelled like him—like soap and skin and boy. "Thank you."

Matthew sat up and hugged her around the waist. Porter had never hugged her like that, like he was feeling a rush of enthusiasm. "I want you to have it."

Frankie wore the T-shirt the next day, and knew from how people looked at her that everyone knew it

127

was Matthew's. Or had been Matthew's. And it felt good to be in his shirt.

But when she told Zada about it, Zada said "Ugh, Frankie, don't be so retro. I mean, Matthew's a good guy and all, but wearing his T-shirt is like wearing a sign that says 'Property of Matthew Livingston' on your breasts."

"Zada!"

"Well, it is."

"It is not."

"It's like he's marking you."

"On the contrary," Frankie snapped. "He gave me something he loves, something he usually wouldn't want to be without."

"Nah, it's like a dog peeing on a hydrant. He's marking you with his scent."

"Oh, stop it."

"All right. Here's another interpretation. Do you look hot in the T-shirt?" Zada asked. "I'm sure you do."

"Yeah, I think I kind of do," said Frankie, giggling.

"So maybe he wanted to see you in it. Maybe he's dressing you up. Did you think of that, he's dressing you up like a doll?"

"No. If he were dressing me up, I think he'd be dressing me in something other than an old T-shirt."

"Really?"

"Come on. It's a ratty T-shirt."

"Maybe that's what he likes."

"Zada. Maybe it's what he *owned* and wanted to give me. Like a sacrifice."

Zada chuckled. "A sacrifice?"

"If you wanted to take that argument further," said Frankie, "you could say he submitted it to me like an offering to a goddess."

"Now you're being ridiculous."

"No more than you saying he's a dog, the shirt is pee, and I'm a hydrant. You're making a nice happy relationship seem completely *maculate*."

"What?"

"Maculate. Morally blemished."

"Whatever."

"Maybe I'm wearing a meaningful sacrificial offering given to me by Matthew Livingston in tribute to my unbelievable goddesslike qualities."

Zada laughed.

"You see?" continued Frankie. "I listened when you went on and on all summer about feminism. And now I take it and throw it back on you! Twisting your argument until it begs for mercy! The giving of the Superman T-shirt is an act of submission!"

"Okay, okay, you can win. Can we change the subject now?"

"Sure."

"I'm not coming home for Thanksgiving."

"Fine. Can't you just be gruntled that I have a boyfriend and he gave me his T-shirt?"

There was a pause from Zada. "Sure. Yes. I'm gruntled that you have a boyfriend and he gave you his T-shirt. Use protection."

"Zada!"

"I'm just saying. There are free condoms at the Planned Parenthood in town; you can walk in and take a handful if you want."

"We've been going out less than four weeks!"

"I'm just saying."

"I'm fifteen!"

"All right. Whatever. Maybe Berkeley is warping me."

"Seems like it."

"Frankie?"

"Yeah?"

"Don't let him erase you, though."

"What?"

"Don't let him erase you," said Zada. "That's what I mean about the shirt."

"Don't worry," said Frankie. "I'm indelible."

The Suicide Club

HE MONDAY after Frankie got the T-shirt, Ms. Jensson—the Cities, Art, and Protest teacher—handed out a stack of photo-copied newspaper and journal articles. They were intended to spur the students toward topics they might select for their term papers. One of the articles was a history of a group of San Franciscans who called themselves "The Suicide Club."

The club got its name from a collection of Robert Louis Stevenson short stories that describe a small, select society in which the members have all agreed to kill themselves. They are desperate men—but they also live their remaining days free from social restrictions. The members of SF Suicide Club, which formed more than one hundred years after the stories were published, did not have any plans to commit suicide, though. They just wanted to live with the same kind of lawless glee.

The club later changed its name to the Cacophony Society, and later still to Cacophony 2.0—but it's basically the same thing any way you cut it. Club members free themselves from the sense of surveillance generated by the panopticon. The panopticon makes them feel like they are always being watched, and they are determined to

1. go where they cannot be watched, such as into the sewers.

2. do what that imaginary unseen watcher would never want them to do, such as climb to the top of a bridge; or

3. behave in such unorthodox ways as to infuriate the unseen watcher, and yet technically not break any rules at all, such as by having parties in graveyards, or dressing as clowns for the morning commute.

Club members refuse to abide by certain unwritten rules, and they make people aware of the existence of those rules by breaking them in public situations.

Frankie would later do her term paper on the Suicide Club and the various urban exploration teams it engendered. It was a very good essay and she received an A.

Here, in the interests of full documentation, is a

short excerpt from the paper she turned in to Ms. Jensson on December 5th of her sophomore year.

The activities of the club and its descendents— the Cacophony Society and Cacophony 2.0—can be classified into two categories: urban exploration and public ridiculousness. As urban explorers, they climbed suspension bridges, most notably the Golden Gate. They infiltrated abandoned buildings and dragged themselves down into the sewer system for an unofficial tour. They threw costume parties in cemeteries.

As publicly ridiculous persons, they would dress in animal costumes and go bowling. One of their more notorious events was "Clowns on a Bus," in which dozens of seemingly unrelated clowns, each waiting at different bus stops on the same route, would board a city bus as part of the morning commute (Santarchy Web site, LA Cacophony Web site).

Another such event is "The Brides of March," which has happened annually for the past eight years. Participants wear wedding dresses and parade the streets buying pregnancy kits, flirting with the clerks in formal-wear stores, shopping at Tiffany's, and trying on lingerie at Victoria's Secret. They finish by drinking champagne at a bar, where they plan to "proposition tourists until we get married or thrown out" (Brides of March Web site).

Club members have been known to spend entire weekends dressed as Santa Claus. The first "SantaCon"—also sometimes called "Santarchy"—was intended as a surreal celebration, a kind of holiday prank. It happened in 1994; people sang naughty versions of Christmas carols and paraded through the streets. It was such a success that its organizers thought it was too perfect to repeat, but they subsequently adopted the motto, "Anything worth doing is worth driving into the ground" (Santarchy Web site).

Now SantaCon is staged in approximately thirty cities; some of the events raise money for charity, others are more about barhopping. The main point is not a critique of the commercialization of Christmas, though some critics have viewed it as such. The main point is the same as that of the Suicide Club and the Cacophony Society: to create psychedelic moments in life, where the usual strictures of society melt away.

When the Portland Santas were evicted from a shopping mall, they chanted "Ho, ho, ho! We won't go!" and "Being Santa is not a crime." When the police threatened them, they cried, "One, two, three . . . Merry Christmas!" Then they ran away and hopped a train downtown, where they all went out for Chinese food (Palahnuik 142).

Many of the club's adventures do go beyond the merely surreal or prankish, into social critique. One fairly recent event, Klowns Against Commerce, tested how much a clown could abuse business people in downtown Los Angeles before he was arrested or beaten up. Another event, a Pigeon Roast sponsored by the fictitious Bay Area Rotisserie Friends was promoted with a gag handout that nevertheless criticizes factory farming and genetic modification (Rotisserie Friends pamphlet).

Both Brides of March and SantaCon take sacred symbols of time-honored institutions—wedding gowns represent the institution of marriage, and Santa represents Christmas—and turn them upside down.

The urban explorations are challenges to those unwritten rules about the use of public buildings and services. You must not play in the cemetery. You must not climb the bridge. You must not enter the tunnels underneath the streets.

Members of the Suicide Club do all these things.

And what is more of a social critique than that?

Frankie later burned her paper, for reasons that will become obvious. This time she was careful to do it in the dormitory shower, and she did not injure herself.

Monster

RANKIE WAS DELIBERATELY a few minutes late to meet Porter for lunch on Wednesday. E-mailing him had brought back a wave of insecurity that she hadn't felt since last year. In the first few days after the breakup, Frankie had been tormented by the idea that Bess must have been better than she was. Ordinary, pleasant Bess must be prettier, more charming, more experienced, smarter than Frankie—or Porter wouldn't have cheated.

It didn't matter that Bess hadn't become Porter's girlfriend after the incident.

It didn't matter that in her heart Frankie knew she was smart and charming.

What mattered was that feeling of being expendable. That to Porter, she was a nobody that could easily be replaced by a better model—and the better model wasn't even so great.

Which meant that Frankie herself was nearly worthless.

It was a bad, inconsequential feeling, and every word of every e-mail Frankie had sent to Porter had been fighting against it. She had made him apologize in more ways than one, had flung neglected positives at him, criticized his grammar—and made him wait for her to accept his invitation. All because of how bad she felt when she remembered how little she'd mattered to him.

The Front Porch snack bar was a canteen for students who wanted to spend money rather than eat in the caf. It had an old-fashioned front porch, but inside, it was nothing but a burger shack; you could buy hamburgers, chicken patty sandwiches, fries, sodas, milk shakes, and ice-cream sundaes. There was a rack of candy bars and a cooling unit full of juice drinks. Every couple years, students would petition for a wider range of options both at the Front Porch and at the caf, requesting veggie burgers, fruit Popsicles, and baked potatoes at the Porch, and some actual vegetables in the salad bar at the caf—sometimes for health reasons, sometimes to promote sustainable agriculture. But the only concession made so far was a bowl of sad-looking apples near the cash register.

In any case, students could pick up a paper plate full of greasy food and either eat it inside with the heat and sizzle of the grill, or take it outside to the screened-in porch.

When Frankie got there, Porter was sitting out front with two orders of cheese fries. Of course it wasn't the first time she'd seen him this year. She saw him all the time; she even had geometry with him. But it was the first time she'd done anything but try to avoid him, and when he stood, she felt small and childish next to his bulk.

"Hey, thanks for coming out," he said.

"Sure, are these mine?" Frankie reached out and snagged a cheese fry, then took the seat opposite Porter.

"Yeah. I wasn't sure what you'd want to drink."

"Have they got that pink lemonade?"

"I'll check."

He popped indoors and came out a few minutes later carrying a bottle of pink lemonade and a can of Viva root beer.

Frankie wished she hadn't ordered pink lemonade.

Pink lemonade was the most infantile drink she could have asked for.

"So what's new?" Frankie asked.

Porter leaned back in his chair. He had a decidedly less geeky look than he'd had when they had started going out. New haircut. Shirt untucked. "Lacrosse is going good," he said. "The Spy Club is deteriorating now that Buckingham graduated."

Frankie nodded.

"You're blowing off the Conglomerate party on Friday for your senior boyfriend, I hear," Porter teased.

"How did you know I had a senior boyfriend?"

"Come on, Frankie, everyone knows."

"Do they?"

"Sure. One of the geeks' own lifted from obscurity by the big man on campus."

"It's not like that." Porter's description made Frankie feel defensive. Was that how people saw her? Lifted out of obscurity by a popular senior boy? Her entire social standing conferred upon her by Matthew?

It probably was.

Because of course, it was pretty much true.

But was that how Matthew saw her?

"So you and Livingston are serious?" Porter was asking.

"Yeah," said Frankie. "I think so."

"He's a lot older."

"So?"

"So." Porter ate a fry and leaned back in his chair. "You look great this year, Frankie. Don't let him take advantage of you."

"Excuse me?"

"You know."

"No, what?"

"Don't let him take advantage."

"Is this what you wanted to discuss?"

Porter scratched his neck. "Kind of. Yeah."

"Tell me you're not saying what I think you're saying."

"What?" His face looked innocent. "It's not anything against you. Or against him. I'm a concerned citizen."

"Why does the way I look make you think I'm suddenly going to let someone take advantage of me?" snapped Frankie. "You never used to think stuff like that about me. I never let *you* take advantage of me."

"No, but—"

"Really, when have I ever been someone it was easy to take advantage of?"

"Um—"

"I mean, easy to cheat on, yes, I see that. You've given me ample evidence of that, thanks very much. But have I ever been easy to take advantage of?"

"Um—"

"Huh, Porter? Answer me."

"Never."

"So?"

"Livingston," sputtered Porter. "He's—"

"What?"

"Like I said, older. And you're . . ."

"What? You sent me all those e-mails and made a plan and everything to tell me something you want to say, so out with it."

"You're so pretty now, Frankie. It's a compliment."

"And what do you mean when you say 'take advantage,' anyway? Like you're assuming guys want something girls don't want? Maybe we want it, too. Maybe Matthew should worry about *me* taking advantage of *him*."

"Don't jump all over me. I was trying to look out for you."

"You think that you saying 'be careful' is going to make the difference between Matthew getting down my pants or not?" Frankie knew she was being harsh, but she was angry. "Like I'm going to be in the middle of making out with him and think, 'Oh, wait, Porter reminded me that I might be getting taken advantage of right now, wow, what a big help, I think I'll go home'?"

"Can you keep your voice down? People are looking at us."

It was true. They were.

Frankie lowered her voice and spat out: "Porter. Let me break it to you. When I am fooling around with Matthew, I am not thinking about you. At all."

"Whoa, Frankie. That is not what I meant."

"So what did you mean?" barked Frankie. "Did you mean that because my bra size is bigger than it used to be, you think I'm not capable of taking care of myself? Or did you mean you think Matthew is a potential date rapist? Or did you mean to remind me that you're a big man, too, you'll protect me, because you're just as big as Matthew—oooh!"

"What is up, Frankie?" Porter was upset now.

She barreled on. "Or were you telling me, in a roundabout way, that you think I'm slutty for going out with a senior? That I should watch my reputation? What is it you were really trying to say, Porter? Because I'd honestly like to hear it."

"Frankie, I don't know what I said to piss you off, but you are being way oversensitive. I started this off with an apology, if you don't remember."

"I'm not oversensitive. I'm just analyzing your supposedly innocent commentary."

"You're being crazy," said Porter, standing. "I was trying to do you a good turn. For old time's sake."

"Well, don't bother."

Porter walked away. Down the steps, leaving his cheese fries half eaten and his root beer unopened.

When he was out of sight around the corner of a building, Frankie opened Porter's soda and drank half of it without stopping. She fingered the Superman T-shirt underneath her cardigan.

Her mind felt alive, like she had used it in some electric way, uncovering all the *nocuous* layers in Porter's seemingly innocuous statement. "You look great this year, Frankie. Don't let him take advantage of you."

She felt strangely proud of what she'd done. She had been right about what Porter had really meant, she was certain she had been.

But she also knew she'd acted like a monster.

Frankie hadn't *liked* herself while she'd been yelling at Porter—but she had admired herself. For not being the littlest one at the table, like she had been all her childhood, depending on the big people (Senior, her mom, Zada) to make sense of the world for her.

For not pouting or grumbling, moping or whining, for not doing any of those behaviors a person engages in when she takes offense but doesn't feel like she has any way to assert herself.

She admired herself for taking charge of the situation, for deciding which way it went. She admired her own verbal abilities, her courage, her dominance.

So I was a monster, she thought. At least I wasn't someone's little sister, someone's girlfriend, some sophomore, some girl—someone whose opinions don't matter.

Frankie walked to her next class, not looking out for Matthew or Trish or anyone. Just feeling the power surging through her, with all its accompanying guilt, righteousness, joy, and fear.

THE LOYAL ORDER

○

As is already no doubt clear to my read-ers, the Loyal Order of the Basset Hounds was alive and well on the Alabaster cam-pus. And in order to understand the events that follow, you will need to know more about its history.

Rumored to have been started by a young man who later would head the nation's second-largest Irish-American crime syndicate, the Basset order was more benevolent than the Skull & Bones society at Yale, less intellectual and more secret than Phi Beta Kappa, and less goth than the Order of Gimghoul at UNC Chapel Hill. Its members, mostly seniors, were tapped by receiving a mysterious letter inviting them to a secret initiation ceremony.

The society's presence was larger on campus some

years than in others. Frankie had made it through her freshman year without ever noticing the small Basset Hound insignia that had decorated the seal on the golf course party invitation, though in truth it had been rubber-stamped on a number of flyers posted on the message kiosk—flyers written in code. 9/4/11/23/TOP meant that at nine o'clock, at meeting location #4 (the utility closet on the top floor of the Flaherty dorm), on November 23rd, there was a top-priority meeting.

(Of course the members of the Loyal Order could have used e-mail to communicate the times and locations of their meetings, but it was part of their mission as a secret society—as it is part of the mission of most secret societies, actually—not to be entirely secret. To be a mystery about which people know just enough to wonder what else there is to know, so that membership in the society holds a certain cachet. If no one knows anything about the society, it is infinitely less exciting to be a involved in it, right?)

The Basset insignia had also been rubber-stamped, somewhat menacingly, on the dorm room clipboards of several loudmouth senior girls who had sat together one day in the cafeteria, deriding the existence of an all-male secret society (if there was one; they didn't know for certain) at an institution that had been coeducational since 1965.

One morning the previous May, Frankie herself

had inadvertently stumbled upon a Basset meeting—but had misinterpreted it as a crew team bonding activity. Having walked in on Porter and Bess the night before, and having then spent most of the night sobbing on Trish's shoulder and saying she hated Porter but also feeling lonely without him, Frankie had left her dorm at six a.m. to walk down by the pond, a small puddle of water decorated with a footbridge that stood on the edge of the Alabaster campus. There, at 6:14 in the morning, she had seen approximately twenty-five boys—half seniors and half juniors, plus one sophomore boy named Sam—standing on the bridge and dropping pennies into the water.

Frankie stood in the trees and watched them for a moment, wondering what on earth could motivate all those guys to be up before Sunday breakfast at nine. She hadn't wanted to walk past them—she wished to be alone—so she was about to turn and walk away, when Matthew Livingston took his shirt off. Which stopped her.

Then he took the rest of his clothes off.

When he was completely naked, he threw himself into the pond. The rest of the boys followed, except the sophomore, who stayed on the bridge to guard the clothes.

Everyone was silent. If they spoke, they whispered, and mostly they paddled around for a minute, then hauled themselves out of the grubby pond onto land to collect their clothes.

They had forgotten to bring towels, and they swore and rubbed at their limbs with their T-shirts.

Frankie had watched them for a few more minutes. She couldn't help herself.

As soon as one of the seniors glanced in her direction, she'd scurried back behind the trees and across campus to the library.

Most secret societies—at least those you can read about in books or on the Internet—are collegiate. Or adult. They are social clubs, or honor clubs, or clubs committed to some value system—chivalry or equality or excellence. They are like fraternities, only they don't have houses or public identities. In colleges, their memberships are usually local, not national, but the adult ones tend to be more serious and on a larger scale.

We don't know what they actually do. Because they're secret.

The Loyal Order of the Basset Hound had been conceived as a society for the elect among Alabaster students—"elect" meaning those from particularly loyal and moneyed Alabaster families, and meaning also those who were considered cool enough. Many collegiate societies have some notion of excellence that drives their selection process, and certainly no one who was not excellent was admitted as a Basset Hound. But it was a notion of excellence as determined by seventeen-year-old boys, not by teachers and parents, so the entertainment potential of your conversation counted considerably more than your ability to craft a decent essay on World War II, and your excellence on the playing field counted only if your ability to banter in the locker room was equally strong. Family wealth and social class didn't count on the surface. What those factors did was to lend the boys who had them an almost intangible sense of security regarding their places in the world, which often (though not always) led to social dominance, which led to induction in the Loyal Order.

Of course, anything named after a floppy-eared dog with short legs isn't deadly serious. The Skull & Bones society, whatever it does, is no doubt much less ridiculous than the Basset Hounds were. The Bassets did not claim to be fostering social change or academic success. Nor did they conceive of themselves as rebellious in any serious way. Bassets were more focused on how to get beer, how to exit and reenter the dorms without detection, and how to get girls to like them— and yet it would not be wrong to call them powerful.

Being a Basset was very important to these boys because it mediated their relationship to the other social institutions that shaped them—most importantly,

Alabaster. Like Senior Banks, they thought of themselves as Bassets more than they thought of themselves, for example, as tennis players, TV watchers, Caucasians, Protestants, East-Coasters, decent skiers, heterosexuals, and attractive young men—all of which most of them were. The Loyal Order was important because the true agenda of the club, though its members didn't exactly articulate it to themselves, was that it allowed them—they whose position in the world was so completely central—to experience the thrill of rebellion, a glimmer of unconventionality, and plain old naughtiness without risk.

It let them play at being bad. At being different. Without any consequences. It gave them a sense of identity that was separate from the values of the school that shaped them, and it gave them a sense of family when they were away from home. Because really, when they were doing their secret rebellious Basset Hound things (i.e., drinking beer on the golf course) they weren't risking their central status at all. They were bonding with other future world leaders, and it was a bond that would serve them very, very well in the years after graduation.

Each year members of the Loyal Order continued the annual tradition of swearing in their new king and swimming naked in the pond. The new generation of juniors took the Mantle of the Basset into their possession, both literally and figuratively (the mantle was a moth-eaten woolen blanket of a slightly disgusting, Bassety brown color), and they all threw pennies into the South Pond in a symbolic gesture that was sometimes said to represent the loss of one's innocence, and other times argued to represent the pledging of eternal loyalty.

This ritual was the one Frankie had stumbled upon at the end of her freshman year, and it had culminated in the one junior who had been groomed for leadership taking his position as Basset King—and possession of the symbolic china doggie. His duty thenceforth to his fellow members of the Order was to guide them, lead them, order them around, and force them to do his bidding.

The position of Basset King, the year Frankie Landau-Banks interfered with the club's operation, was held by two people. Alpha had been tapped his sophomore year to attend Basset parties and meetings with the understanding that he'd step into Basset King position at the end of his junior year. But then he'd spent that year in New York, and a substitute had to be found, since no one knew at that time that Alpha would be coming back.

That substitute was Matthew Livingston.

A Sea Horse

VERY WEEK, Alabaster screened a film. It was a G-rated series, featuring only selections that could not be deemed objectionable by any of the conservative Old-Boy alums who had donated the money to build the arts complex. One day, midweek in October, Matthew asked if Frankie wanted to go see *The Muppet Movie* on Friday.

"None of the guys. Just me and you, Miss Piggy, and a giant pack of Twizzlers," Matthew said. "I'll pick you up and we can walk over together." They hadn't been on many dates that didn't involve an entourage of boys going with them.

Trish (Debate Club) and Artie (Debate, AudioVisual/ Technology Club) were spending Friday night at this year's Geek Club Conglomerate party. "You have to go!" wailed Trish, when Frankie told her about *The Muppet Movie*. "You're like the heroine of the alliance; you're the whole reason the debaters even get invited."

"I know, I know," answered Frankie. "But think about it: candy, a boyfriend, a darkened theater? Or a bunch of geeks doing the macarena semi-ironically?"

"No, think of it this way," said Trish. "Plastic chewy things that aren't even food, the same guy you hang around with every day, and a movie that's basically a puppet show for five-year-olds, versus an awesome DJ, unlimited potato chips, and all your friends."

"They're not puppets, they're Muppets," said Frankie. "I have a serious and justified love for Kermit that I will parage to the end."

"Parage?"

"Parage. The neglected positive of disparage."

"You mean defend. You will defend Kermit to the end."

"Parage."

"Praise?"

"Parage. I will parage him. And Animal, too. I love Animal. I used to watch that show on DVD all the time when I was little."

Trish changed the subject. "We should do facials and paint our toenails Friday before they pick us up. What do you say, blow through dinner and come back here for girlie stuff?"

Frankie said, "You're on. When we're finished, we'll be absolutely sheveled."

"You'll be sheveled," said Trish. "I'm a normal person."

That evening, Frankie walked into dinner alone. Her modern dance class had been cut short for an unimportant reason.

She had not, she realized, been alone in the caf since the start of sophomore year. She always came in to breakfast with Trish or some other girls on her hall, and went to lunch either with Matthew or with a couple of Debate Club kids who had fifth period with her. Sometimes she went to dinner with Trish and Artie and sat at the sophomore tables, but usually, since dance got out before soccer anyway, she picked up Matthew and his friends outside the new gymnasium.

This day, Frankie was hungry and went as soon as the dining hall opened. But when she got through the line with her tray of eggplant Parmesan and apple juice, she stood alone, unsure where she belonged.

Trish and Artie were at the sophomore tables, and so were some other people she knew.

The senior table where Matthew and his friends always sat—was empty.

Frankie glanced at the clock and figured he wouldn't be there for another ten minutes.

She knew she was supposed to go sit with the sophomores. She was only entitled to sit at the senior tables when a senior invited her. There were no *official* school rules about who sat where in the caf, but no underclassman—no junior, even—had sat at a senior table unaccompanied by a senior since 1958.

Frankie wanted to sit with Matthew and Alpha and their friends. Not just because she liked being with them, but because sitting at the sophomore tables would be like accepting that her status was not equal to Matthew's. That she wasn't really friends with his friends.

It would also be bowing to the pressures of the panopticon Ms. Jensson talked about. To sit with Trish and Artie would be conforming to unwritten rules for fear of discovery by a nonexistent watchman.

No one is going to punish me, Frankie told herself.

I can break this rule if I want.

Nothing can actually stop me.

Frankie walked deliberately over to Matthew's table and sat down. As if she owned it. As if she had any right to be there.

She sat, and ate.

She read some of *Eggs, Beans and Crumpets* by P. G. Wodehouse. Artie and Trish called her name and waved her over, but she chose to misunderstand them, and just waved back to say hello.

No one spoke to her, although there were several

seniors at neighboring tables whom she knew fairly well from sitting near them regularly. Callum sat down at the table next to her with a bunch of other guys from lacrosse, and didn't even nod.

She ate, and read.

There was a part of Frankie that felt what nearly any teenager would have felt in that situation: embarrassed. She wished she hadn't broken this stupid rule. She wished Matthew would come and rescue her. She felt desperate and sad that Callum hadn't spoken to her, because it was proof that he and those other guys didn't rate her as a person but only as Matthew's arm candy. Maybe she should walk over and sit with Trish after all—only, if she got up now it would be even more embarrassing, and *why on earth had she done such a dumb thing?*

But another part of Frankie enjoyed the fact that she'd made herself a subject of discussion. That she'd broken a rule so entrenched in everybody's mind that it never occurred to anyone that it wasn't actually a rule. That she had defied the sense of surveillance created by the panopticon of her boarding school.

Finally, Matthew, Alpha, and Dean arrived along with Star and Elizabeth. They sat down with a clatter of trays and began unloading glasses of juice and milk. Alpha jumped up for napkins. Dean ran to a nearby table for salt.

It was only Elizabeth who made any commentary on where Frankie was sitting. She was the outsider, the one who had earned her own money, the one unfettered by the privileged class's sense of "noblesse oblige"—the feeling Bertie Wooster always references in the Wodehouse novels, that along with noble birth comes an obligation to treat others well. "Taking over the senior table, eh, squirt?" teased Elizabeth, not unkindly, sitting next to Frankie and unloading a tray filled with many small saucers of discrete items from the salad bar—canned beets, canned mushrooms, pimento olives, and raisins, plus a toasted English muffin with butter and two glasses of juice.

"Maybe," said Frankie, her defenses up. "Or maybe I was pining away for Matthew and waiting for him like a lonesome puppy. It's hard to tell from the outside, isn't it?"

Elizabeth raised her eyebrows. "You have some balls."

Frankie hated that expression, ever since Zada had pointed out to her that it equates courage with the male equipment, but she nodded at Elizabeth and said, "Some days I do."

"What do you think, Livingston?" Elizabeth asked Matthew. "Your girlie waiting for you at the senior tables?"

Matthew stood and leaned across the table to

stroke Frankie's cheek. "I'm always glad to see Frankie."

"Mushball," muttered Alpha.

"Lay off. I touched her cheek."

"You're a complete ball of mush, my dog."

"Be nice about me, Alpha," said Frankie, not liking the way the conversation was going. "I'm sitting right here."

"I wouldn't mind if Dean was a mushball," said Star, sulky.

"No disparagement upon your person, Frankie." Alpha stuffed a large piece of eggplant into his mouth. "Your person is young and lovely and we're always glad to see you. It's the mush when I'm eating, little lady. It puts me off my feed."

"I didn't start the mush," Frankie argued. "Matthew started the mush. I was minding my own business." She felt like she was ten again, the youngest at the dinner table, trying to keep out of trouble.

"Alpha, we went over this already," said Matthew, looking down at his pasta.

When? When had they gone over what, exactly?

"We went over it," said Alpha, pausing to take a sip of coffee. "But we didn't *finish* going over it."

"Now is not the time or place." Matthew kept his head down.

They had been arguing about her, Frankie was

159

sure. Why did Alpha always call Matthew away when she and Matthew were together? Was Alpha jealous of Matthew being with Frankie—or of Frankie being with Matthew? Or did Alpha just not *like* her? Or like her too much?

"Boys." Elizabeth rolled her eyes. "That extra dose of testosterone makes them unbearable, don't you think?"

"What, you mean testosterone like the hormone?" asked Star.

"No, the other kind of testosterone," put in Alpha, snorting.

Star looked perplexed.

Frankie shrugged. "I'm not sure it's about testosterone."

"Sure it is," argued Elizabeth. "Boys have got oceans of it hurtling around in their systems. It makes them needlessly aggressive. Like these two, they're like moose locking antlers right now."

"I don't think you can blame it on testosterone," put in Alpha. "No one's getting violent, here. What we're getting is testy."

"And that's exactly my point," said Elizabeth. "Testosterone, testy. The words even have the same origin, I bet."

"No they don't," said Matthew. "They don't, actually."

"Anyways, I disagree." Alpha waved his piece of eggplant at Elizabeth. "Testosterone is making me horny, and the consequences of *that* you can deal with later, but the thing that's making me annoyed with Matthew is not testosterone."

"What is it, then?" Elizabeth picked up a cucumber in her fingers and ate it.

"It's Matthew."

"Ha. You two are a pair of moose, having a contest to see who's got the biggest set of horns. Are you with me, Frankie? Star?"

"Absolutely," said Star, taking a bite of toast. "They're animals."

Frankie knew she was expected to side with Elizabeth, but she didn't agree. "I think girls can be as competitive as boys," she said.

"Come on," said Elizabeth. "Look at nature. Who's got the big tail, the peacock or the—what's it?"

"Peahen," said Matthew.

"Exactly. And who's got the big horns? The shaggy mane?" asked Elizabeth.

"The boys," answered Dean.

"Yeah, yeah," said Frankie. "But lions are a good example of what I'm saying, actually. The female lions do all the gazelle hunting while the males sit around and, I don't know, roar. The women are fiercer than the men."

161

"Oh, no." Elizabeth turned to look at Frankie. "Because what do they do after they kill the gazelle? They give it to the guy lion. And they all stick together, it's like all about lady lion sisterhood, whereas the males are lone rangers. They don't hang around with each other because they're too combative, but the females are all about cooperation."

"Yay for the lady lions!" said Star. "Sisterhood is so important."

But Frankie said, "That's a slippery slope to be heading down, Elizabeth."

"Why?"

"Because once you say women are one way, and men are another, and say that's how it is in other species so that's gotta be how it is in people, then even if it's somewhat true—even if it's quite a good amount true— you're setting yourself up to make all kinds of assumptions that actually really suck. Like, women tend to cooperate with each other and therefore don't have enough competitive drive to run major companies or lead army squadrons. Or men are inherently unfaithful because they want to propagate their seed. Assumptions like these do nothing but cause problems in the world."

"Ooh," said Elizabeth. "The underclassman debater rears her fierce head."

"Besides which, you can read a situation several different ways. If it was the female pea . . . ?"

"Peafowl," said Matthew.

"Peafowl that had the blue tail, everyone would be saying it was all about how girls are more beautiful than guys, girls are more concerned with appearance, girls like all that gaudy, froufrou stuff—"

"Girls are definitely more beautiful," interrupted Dean.

"Thank you, sweetie." This from Star.

"Maybe in some species, but not in peafowl. That's my point," said Frankie. "In peafowl, it's the boys that are more beautiful, and then we call it testosterone. Manliness instead of prettiness. Do you see what I'm saying?"

"I get your point," said Elizabeth snidely. "We all get your point. But what I'm saying is that these guys ragging on each other is the same as a pair of peacocks fanning out their tails, each one going, 'Hey, dogs, check out my tail, aren't I a man's man?' The way that some guys flash their wallets. And girls don't do that."

"Aren't you two doing it now?" asked Alpha.

Frankie ignored him. "I'm saying, once you start saying women are all about sisterhood and community, then you start underestimating people who might easily, I don't know, take over the world."

"Ooh, very Oprah."

"Same with men," said Frankie. "Once you say they're all about testosterone, even if that's partway true, you make them think they've all *got* to be about testosterone. Then the untestosteroney guys, the . . . what is that fish? Which fish is it that the man one carries the babies?"

"Sea horse," said Matthew, still looking down at his plate.

"Yes, so then the sea horses of the world feel like they have to be the moose of the world, and no one gives respect to the sea horses, and you have misery. Don't you?"

Alpha finished eating and pushed his plate to the center of the table. "I would like to assert," he said solemnly, "that if Matthew were an animal he would be a sea horse."

"Dog," said Matthew, shaking his head. "I am not a sea horse."

"Aren't you? Because you act like a sea horse."

"What's wrong with a sea horse?" asked Frankie. "I know a lot of girls who would love a sea horse."

"See?" Alpha waved his hand toward Frankie. "That's precisely my point."

"What?" asked Frankie.

"Alpha," Matthew's voice was stern. "Didn't I say we'd go over this later?"

(What were they going over? Something to do with her. With Alpha's objections to her.)

"Fine," said Alpha, standing. He looked for a

moment as if he were going to depart in a huff. But then he seemed to change his mind, and walked around to where Elizabeth was sitting and whispered loudly: "Eat up your raisins and let's discuss my testosterone situation alone, what do you say?"

Elizabeth shook her head. "I'm doing college essays with Hannah and Rosemary after dinner. You have to deal with your testosterone by yourself, mister."

"Harsh," muttered Dean.

"Oh, she tries to whip me," laughed Alpha. "She tries with all her evil machinations. But I'm unwhippable."

"Hardly," Elizabeth said.

"It's true," said Alpha, waving over his shoulder as he left the caf. "Immune to the whip, that's me."

Elizabeth stayed for only a minute after Alpha disappeared. Then she collected her many saucers onto her tray and took off.

"You think she's following him?" Frankie asked Matthew. She had heard Alpha talk about sex like that before, like he was having it, he'd always had it, like he'd never been a virgin and sex was no big thing. But it disconcerted her every time he did it.

"They always follow Alpha," smirked Dean. "No matter how loud they talk, how much they squawk, the she-wolf always follows in the end."

* * *

165

When they walked out together, Matthew betrayed no reaction to Frankie having sat alone at a senior table. And no reaction either to the debate with Elizabeth or Alpha's sea horse comment. Except—he didn't mention them. Now that Frankie thought of it, Matthew had pretty much stayed out of the conversation when it happened—quite unusual for a guy whose idea of a friendly mealtime chat was to argue abortion politics or Middle East policy.

He had never asked about her lunch date with Porter, either.

As they strolled toward the dorms, Matthew babbled about his college applications (Yale, Princeton, Harvard, Brown, etc.), questioned Frankie about her ultimate game on Saturday, told a funny story about having been a fried egg for Halloween and getting chased by a big kid who was a fork.

"What did you mean when you said to Alpha that you'd go over something later?" Frankie asked, gently interrupting him.

"Oh, nothing."

"'Cause it sounded like it was about me. Like Alpha has some problem with *me*."

"Are you kidding?" Matthew said, his smile spreading tightly across his face. "Alpha thinks you're great. He's just spouting off. Don't be so sensitive, okay?" Then he announced he had a calculus study session, kissed her in front of her dorm, and headed off into the evening.

Something was wrong. Frankie could feel it.

Maybe she was going to be punished for sitting at that table, after all.

STAR

HE NEXT MORNING, Star grabbed Frankie's shoulder, coming out of history. "Can I talk to you?"

"Um, sure." Frankie waved good-bye to Trish and walked with Star to a bench, where they sat down.

"Dean and I broke up," Star blurted, her face contorting. "I mean, it happened last night after dinner. I thought everything was going great, we were going out, la-la-la, it was all fine, and then he breaks up with me."

Frankie said the only thing one can say in such situations: "Shocker. You seemed so happy together." But she wondered, Why is Star telling *me*? Why doesn't she cry to Claudia, or Ash, or Catherine, one of her real friends who actually likes her?

"It's like he changed his mind all of a sudden, and I don't know why. And I thought I was okay last night, I did, but then there I was at breakfast this morning, and none of them talked to me, Frankie. I mean, not even Elizabeth. She didn't even say one thing to me and I was right next to her, you know at the table where you can toast your English muffins?"

"What did she do?"

"I said hello and she didn't answer. Then I said I guess she heard about me and Dean, but not to worry, it was a mutual decision. She just nodded like she already knew that wasn't true, and walked away." Star sniffed. "Then Claudia picked this table—she acts so smart but inside she's so dumb sometimes, you know?—Claudia picked this table that meant I had to walk by them all to get to her, and so I thought, Okay Star, you have to have dignity, you've gotta do it. And I went by—after sitting at that table every morning since the start of school—I went by and nobody spoke. Dean wasn't even there, but nobody said a word, not even hello, good morning. Nothing."

"Wow."

"It was like I'd never been their friend, like they didn't even see me."

"So cold."

"I mean, how can you hang out with people every day for like two months and then one morning they don't know you exist? I mean, *really* don't know you, Frankie. It's not like they had decided to ignore me. You know how it feels when someone is ignoring you. You can feel they know you're there. This was like they didn't register me as a person they had ever known."

"Do you want me to talk to them?"

Star shook her head. "I just thought maybe Dean or someone had spoken to you about why he broke up with me? Or did he ever complain about me when I wasn't there?"

"No."

"You seem much more in with them than me. Matthew respects you. And Alpha does, too."

No, they don't, Frankie thought. But instead she said: "I didn't see Dean or any of those guys this morning. I ate breakfast with Trish."

"Matthew didn't say anything to you last night?"

"I don't think guys talk to each other about stuff like that. Not right after it happens. Not in detail. Dean probably didn't even tell him."

Star wiped her eyes. "Maybe not. But will you let me know if you hear anything?"

Frankie nodded, but she wasn't thinking about Star.

She was thinking how easy it would be for the same thing to happen to her.

A BROKEN DATE

THAT FRIDAY, after an early dinner, Frankie and Trish put mud packs on their faces and painted their nails. They put girlie pop music on the portable CD player and took turns fanning each other's toes with a copy of Trish's *Horse Illustrated* magazine.

"You can still apologize to Porter if you feel bad about what happened," Trish said, admiring her toenails. "But I don't think he's mad at you, anyhow."

"Oh, he's mad at me, all right," said Frankie.

"I think he's mad at Matthew for being better than he is. He doesn't like how small he feels when he compares himself to your new boyfriend." (In addition to *Horse Illustrated*, Trish subscribed to *Psychology Today*.)

"Whatever. It's not like Porter likes me anymore, anyway."

"Maybe he does." Trish wrinkled her brow. "I mean, why wouldn't he? He never stopped liking you. He just cheated on you."

"Same thing."

"No, not the same thing at all. If Porter liked Bess, he would have started going out with her. But he didn't. And now he's sending you e-mails and XO-ing you and buying you cheese fries."

"So?"

"So if that's not flirting, I don't know what is."

"I'm not apologizing to him," said Frankie. "The guy is completely maculate."

"I'm not even going to ask you what that means." Trish rolled her eyes.

"A little flirting doesn't make up for what he did."

"I'm not saying you should apologize," Trish answered. "I'm just pointing out that more is going on here than meets the eye. There are layers and layers."

"Okay." Frankie was sarcastic.

"I think the question is *not* whether Porter is mad at you," Trish continued. "The question is, what made you so mad at Porter? Was it the cheating thing from last year, or the Big Man Protector thing he did at lunch, or the fact that he was flirting with you when you have a boyfriend, and that made you all confused?"

"I don't know. I couldn't stand his superior attitude."

"He was always that way." Trish tucked the bottle of sparkly green polish into her bureau drawer and threw her cotton balls in the trash.

"Was he? I don't remember."

"I mean, Porter's not a bad guy, except for the cheating," said Trish, "but he does have that James Bond thing going with women."

"What do you mean, Bond?"

Trish shook her head. "Give me a goofball like Artie any day. I don't need all that macho-rescue stuff. I just like someone funny who treats me nice."

Artie was a sweetheart, but Frankie found him completely devoid of sexual appeal. "He's a good boyfriend," she told Trish. "You're lucky."

"Did I tell you he wants to be a girl for Halloween?" said Trish, combing her hair in the mirror.

"You're kidding."

"Yeah, he and John and Charles Deckler are already borrowing people's panty hose."

Frankie murmured something in response, but she was no longer paying attention. Talking about Porter had reminded her that she was nervous about her date.

Matthew had been so atypically silent when Frankie had debated Elizabeth.

Had she embarrassed him?

Or turned him off?

Or annoyed him by sitting at the senior table, though he was much too polite to ever say so?

Alpha had been calling Matthew a sea horse. Implying he was whipped.

Frankie put on perfume, which she almost never wore.

She changed her shirt.

A pebble pinged at their window. "Matthew's out there," Trish said, looking down.

"Geek it up tonight," Frankie told Trish, grabbing her coat.

"I will."

Matthew was standing at the foot of the steps with his hands behind his back. "I have to talk to you," he said.

"What?"

"Come here. Walk with me."

"Okay."

They strolled across the quad, and he took her hand. "I can't take you to the movie tonight, Frankie."

"Oh."

"I'm sorry, I should have told you earlier."

"What's happened?"

"It's not a big deal. I just can't go; I've got something else I have to do."

"Something with Alpha?" she asked.

Matthew nodded.

"He's making you change plans?"

"Not making me, exactly. He reminded me of an obligation. There's somewhere I gotta be."

And Alpha doesn't want me there, Frankie thought. But I don't want to let Alpha make the rules. "Can't you take me with you?" she asked.

"No."

"How come? Is someone sick?" She knew no one was sick.

"It's—it's a guy thing, Frankie. You know I'd love to bring you, but Alpha—No, I shouldn't blame him. I agreed to it being a guy thing myself."

Frankie's heart felt cold. She thought, He's angry at me and this is a repercussion. For sitting alone at the senior table, for disagreeing with the she-wolf, for demanding that Alpha be nice to me, or for liking the way sea horse daddies carried their babies—it doesn't matter which, even. When I act the way I acted, Matthew doesn't like me as much as he does when I fall off my bicycle.

Is he breaking up with me?

What can I do? Frankie thought. What can I say?

Is there anything I can say that will make him change his mind?

Don't sound whiny. Don't sound defensive. Don't sound pitiful. Don't sound angry.

I can't say any of the things I feel, because none of them are any good.

Can't say, "But you promised."

Can't say, "I put on makeup. I did my nails, I looked forward to it all day."

Can't say, "Are you breaking up with me?"

I can't lose him.

I can't lose *them*, either.

What will get me what I want?

If she were not a strategist, Frankie would have reacted like most girls do in the same situation: with tears, with anger, with pouting and sulking and petulant responses like "What is it that's so much more important than hanging out with me, huh?" or "Fine, if that's how you're going to be about it, don't talk to me again!" or "You're acting like your time is more valuable than mine." But she was—and is—a strategist, and therefore she considered her options.

Quick analysis revealed she had two goals. First, keep her boyfriend. Second, stop him from putting her in her place, which is what she felt he was trying to do. He was prioritizing something else, and didn't want her to ask, complain, or wonder about it.

Frankie touched the soft skin underneath Matthew's ear, then kissed him gently on the mouth, outlining his lower lip with her tongue. "S'okay. I can go to that Conglomerate party with Trish and Porter and those guys."

It was a mean move, mentioning Porter, and Frankie knew it. "What party?" asked Matthew.

"It's an annual thing," she said, choosing not to explain the geek element. "I went last year. Porter arranged a DJ and Trish helped with the catering."

Matthew looked at her. Was he surprised she had something else to do? Was he jealous of Porter? Had she regained the power?

Frankie leaned in and kissed him again, harder, running her hand up his sweater and across his warm stomach. "I wanted to kiss you in the cold air," she said. "Doesn't it smell like Halloween?"

He nodded.

"I was thinking about kissing you during English class today," she whispered, bringing her lips against his ear. "I was thinking how you look with your shirt off."

Matthew pressed his body against hers and backed her against a tree, looking at her.

He's not breaking up with me, she suddenly knew. She'd gained some ground. She could tell by the way he put his arms around her that he wanted to hold her tight, keep her from the party and her ex-boyfriend.

Frankie looked at Matthew's beautiful face. "Have fun," she told him. "I'll go to that party with Trish."

She didn't mention Porter again. She didn't need to. She'd reversed the power dynamics of the situation to the best of her ability: Matthew now wanted to be with her instead of wherever he was going—and he was insecure about what she'd get up to when he was gone.

Matthew kissed her, pressing his entire body hard against hers in a way he hadn't done before, then ran off into the night.

Frankie waited until Matthew was twenty yards away—and then she followed him.

The Old Theater

ATTHEW MADE A LEFT at the library
and headed across campus. It was dark,
a little before eight p.m., and the paths
were fairly crowded. Kids were heading to Front
Porch, the arts complex, the Geek Conglomerate party,
and other school-sponsored events that kicked off the
weekend. It was easy for Frankie to follow Matthew
without his seeing her. She ditched her pink sweater
on a tree branch, hoping to come back for it later, and
proceeded in her dark T-shirt, black skirt, and brown
boots.

He arrived at the old theater, which had passed for
an arts complex before the new one had been built.
This part of Alabaster was dark after sundown—at
least so long as no school plays were being rehearsed in

the evenings—and there were no lights on. Matthew went around to the side of the building that was deep in shadow, climbed onto a folding chair that stood under a tree, pulled himself up into the tree, slid through a window, and was gone.

Frankie ducked into a shadow beneath the stairs of a neighboring building and watched as Callum, Dean, Steve, and Tristan, one by one, entered the theater.

When it seemed certain no more boys were coming, Frankie climbed the tree. She peeked into the second-floor window and climbed through into a storage room for lighting equipment. Piles of lights and gels and extension cords lined the walls on either side. Light came through the window, but the hall before her was nearly black.

Frankie peeked around the corner and saw no one, caught no shadow of movement. At some distance, she could hear voices and the clink of bottles.

She felt her way down the hall and found a stair-case. Heading down, stepping as quietly as she could, she came out in the lobby of the theater—a small, somewhat shabby room with a marble floor. Two sets of double doors led to the auditorium. She pressed her ear against one of them—yes, the boys were in there.

On the other side of the lobby was a second stair-well. Frankie eased up it, heart pounding, then felt her way in the darkness down that hall to the back of the building, past drama teacher offices and storage, down another set of steps, until she found herself where she wanted to be. In the wings.

She could see here. Someone had turned a few red lights on, illuminating the stage, and from the dark curtains she could see out into the audience.

Only there was no one there.

Frankie shivered. She was sure Dean or someone would pop out from behind the velvet curtains and . . . she wasn't sure what.

Make her feel small. Make her feel like no one.

A moment later, Alpha's voice came from above. They were in the catwalks—a group of three narrow platforms high above the stage, used for dropping fake snow, arranging lights, hauling set-pieces up and down. The boys were sitting on two of the walkways, facing each other with their legs hanging down. They leaned their chests on the spindly railings.

"I hereby call to order the Loyal Order of the Basset Hounds," Alpha intoned.

"Sorry." It was Matthew's voice talking to the assembled group. "We gotta find something better to say than 'call to order the loyal order.'"

"We've been saying it this way for decades, dog," retorted Alpha.

"So?"

"So, it's the thing that is said. To convene a Basset meeting."

"It's still bad."

"You have *got* to kill your inner copy editor."

Matthew ignored him. "Let's proceed. Does everyone who wants a beer have a beer?"

"Yes, oh Basset Kings."

"And does everyone who wants soda have soda?" he confirmed.

"Yes, oh Basset Kings."

"And there are chips, let me see, um, ranch and barbeque," Matthew announced. "Callum, toss 'em out."

Callum threw bags of chips from one catwalk platform to the other. The boys—there were eleven of them—caught them easily.

"No dribbling your beer, no dropping chip crumbs, do you hear me, dogs?" said Alpha.

"Yes, oh Basset Kings."

"Because if some early morning drama students find bits of barbeque chip on the floor of the stage tomorrow," Alpha explained, "we're gonna end up with increased security in this building. They've already alarmed the door to the roof of Talbot, thanks to you nimrods smoking up there."

"Yes, oh Basset Kings."

"All righty then. The oath," said Alpha, and the boys began to chant:

Atop the crown of Alabaster,
Bind it tight with sticking plaster.
Look to the west, boys;
Look to the books, men!
History is our guide!
Keep the secrets, tunnel under,
Climb the heights, our pack defend.
The Basset is a hardy beast,
We vow our loyalty to the end.

Their voices rang out across the hollow space of the theater, and Frankie could feel the weight of their commitment as they chanted. She looked up through the red light, trying to see which boys were there (besides those she'd seen go in), but the angle was so strange and the light so dim that she couldn't make out their faces well.

When they finished chanting, they all banged their drinks on the floors of the catwalks three times, then drank.

"We've called this meeting to figure out what to do on Halloween," announced Alpha. "That's next Friday. Livingston, tell me what we did last year."

"A large pumpkin was carved with the shape of a Basset Hound and placed in front of the headmaster's office."

"What?"

"That's what we did," admitted Matthew.

"That sucks." Alpha was aghast.

"Yeah."

"That's worse than the year before!"

"That was a basset hound?" asked Dean. "On the pumpkin?" Unlike Matthew and Alpha, he and the other seniors hadn't been Basset Hounds until late spring of their junior year. "There was no way to tell that was supposed to be a basset. Seriously, it looked like a blob. I saw that pumpkin in the hallway, and was like, what the—?"

"I never even saw it," said Callum.

"Me neither."

"Me neither."

"Who goes by Richmond's office anyway, unless they can help it?"

"Do you think he even knew what it meant?"

"Okay, okay," said Matthew. "It was Hogan's idea. He read something on the Internet about these amazing carved pumpkins and got all craftsy on us. He thought it would be a real coup, you know, like 'The Bassets have been here!'—only, yeah, no one saw it, and the people who did see it didn't know what it was. Not one of our best efforts."

"The year before," explained Alpha, "we got glow-in-the-dark paint and painted the Guppy." A three-foot-long statue of an unidentified fish, commonly known as "the Guppy," stood proudly on the front lawn of the school.

"That was us?" Callum nearly squealed. "I loved that."

"It just, like, started glowing as the sun went down. It was good," said Alpha.

"But Callum was your roommate sophomore year, and if even he didn't know, that's a problem," said Matthew. "Don't we want to make a mark people can actually recognize? 'Cause if two years down the line, no one's even talking about the Halloween prank as anything to do with the Basset Hounds, then there's not much point. We should be creating a legend."

"I agree," said Alpha. "Dean's girlfriend thought the hound on the invitations was a Snoopy. We've got to change that."

"She's not my girlfriend anymore," Dean objected.

"I move that if we can't think of anything really good," said Matthew, "there's not a lot of point to doing *anything* on Halloween. We could just meet here and drink beer."

"Fine by me," said Callum.

"No, you nimrods," said Alpha. "We have to do a prank. Basset Hounds always do a prank on Halloween. It's a tradition."

"Since when?" asked Tristan.

"I have no idea. Since at least two years ago when I joined, okay? It's not like that movie *The Skulls*, where everyone gets a supposedly top-secret rule book with their name embossed on the cover. There's no written history, no handbook."

"All right, I get it." Callum sounded annoyed.

Frankie's mind reeled. Because she knew.

There *was too* a handbook.

Senior and Hank Sutton and Dr. Montague had told her and Zada about it at the steak house. *The Disreputable History.*

Why didn't Alpha know about it?

Where could it be?

"We're a seat-of-the-pants operation, dogs," Alpha continued. "But we gotta get a prank going for Halloween, that's clear. Something awesome and destructive, something that'll build the legend of the Hounds. Are we in agreement?"

"Yes, oh Basset King."

"Matthew?" asked Alpha.

"Agreed."

"Good."

"Oh, and our youngest members?" added Matthew. "You, as tradition demands, will have the honor of executing whatever we decide."

"Why them?" asked Callum.

"They have the least to lose if they get caught. No college applications."

"Harsh."

"Not harsh, my dog," said Alpha. "Fair. It's part of

showing your worthiness to ascend to the kingship next year, and it's a way of getting the backs of the kings who went before you."

"So did you carve that dumb pumpkin?" Callum asked Sam, the junior.

"Me and Matthew," said Sam.

"And you painted the Guppy sophomore year, right?" Matthew asked Alpha, though clearly he already knew the answer.

"I most certainly did. Dumped the rest of the glow-in-the-dark paint down the boys' john, where late-night tinkles glowed phosphorescent for nearly a month afterward. Nearly plopped myself thinking someone was going to notice the stuff under my fingernails."

"Okay, then," said Matthew. "Whatever we decide on, it'll be executed by the two-man team of Sam and Porter, in the traditional show of loyalty to the Order. Understood?"

"Yes, oh Basset King."

Frankie shivered.

The sophomore chosen to be the future King—was Porter.

Matthew must know she'd been lying when she talked about going to the party with Porter. Because he knew where Porter was going that night.

And Porter had a connection to Matthew.

Frankie tried to remember *when* she'd told

Matthew she'd dated Porter—she was sure it had been late September, when they'd been going out only a couple of weeks. They'd sat on the lawn during a free period together and talked about their exes. But the Basset Hounds, they'd had the golf course party at the start of the year—had Porter been there?

He had. She had crossed the green to avoid him, she remembered. So he'd already been a Basset when she and Matthew started going out—and Matthew had been lying when he'd pretended not to know who Porter was.

So why had Porter tried to warn her about Matthew?

Frankie tailed it back to the tree where she'd left her sweater, and from there to the Geek Conglomerate party, where she danced and talked to people as if nothing were on her mind. She felt she needed an alibi.

The Oath

THE NEXT MORNING, Frankie ran into Alpha at the English muffin table—which was mainly inhabited by large loaves of bread and toasters, but that's what everyone called it.

"Morning," he said, like everything was great between them. Like he had never made Matthew cancel his date. He was "Alpha in the Morning," unshaven and scraggle-haired, taking up space just in the way he loaded his tray with breakfast—dashing across the room for butter, calling to the caf lady to please yelp at him when the new bacon came out, drinking his tea while he waited for his toast to pop, balancing his tray under one arm like a football. He was, as she always found him, delightful.

But a small war had been declared, Frankie knew.

For possession of Matthew. For a position at the senior table. For status, really, as the alpha dog.

"Hey," she answered, fork-splitting a muffin and sticking it in a toaster.

Alpha warmed his hands over the orange glow. "You look incredibly fetching today, Frankie."

"Thanks."

"I mean it. You're such a pretty girl. Matthew's a lucky guy."

Was this an apology? Or a reduction of Frankie to the status of Pretty Girl, rather than Serious Competition?

"Well," she said, smiling, "I do brush my hair before I come to breakfast."

Alpha scratched his head. "Yeah, well. It works for you. You coming to sit with us?"

"I got my friend Trish. She's over there, in the red sweatshirt."

"She can come. I want to meet her."

He is smarter than I thought, Frankie realized. He's betting that if he gives me more of what I want, I won't try and take it from him. That if he invites my friends to the table, hangs with me when Matthew's not around, lets me *in* a little more, I'll be so wild about him, them, the whole thing, that I won't take Matthew away. I'll forget to fight.

He's wrong, she thought. But he doesn't have to

know that. "All right," she said, as her toaster popped. "Lemme negotiate the jam situation here and I'll come by."

They ate breakfast—Alpha, Callum, Trish, and Frankie. Matthew and Dean joined them twenty minutes in. Frankie scanned Matthew for signs that he harbored any suspicions of her having lied to him about Porter being at the Geek Conglomerate party—but there was nothing. He just sat there being "Matthew in the Morning," which meant wet-haired and slow-moving, leaning his head on her shoulder and complaining he was still asleep, inviting Trish (now that she had entered his world) to come, hypothetically, over to Martha's Vineyard from Nantucket next summer.

Frankie felt a surge of affection for him. How adorable he was. How generous his spirit. How smart. How funny.

Dean and Alpha bussed their trays, leaving Frankie, Trish, and Matthew alone at the table.

"Hey, how was your party?" Matthew wanted to know.

"Good," Frankie answered. "We danced with the members of the Chess Club. You would not believe what some of those chess boys will do when they get their groove on. And there was a disco ball."

"I'm jealous."

"Of the chess boys or the disco ball?"

Trish rolled her eyes. "You do *not* need to be jealous of the chess boys."

"Maybe." Matthew turned to Frankie. "But didn't you go with your ex-boyfriend, Peter what's-his name?"

"Porter."

Why was he asking? To see if she'd lie?

"Porter, right. He's bigger than I am," Matthew went on. "You always gotta worry when your girlfriend goes to a party with a guy who's bigger than you."

"Porter didn't show," said Frankie.

"I didn't see him, either," said Trish. "Maybe he was sick."

Matthew pouted. "Here I was, all worked up to be jealous that Frankie went out with her ex-boyfriend, and now I got nowhere to put my energies."

"You want to worry about the chess guys instead?" asked Frankie, reaching over and taking a drink of his tea.

"Wow. Maybe I will. Because I've got to live up to what Elizabeth was saying about moose and testosterone."

"Go to town. Those chess guys were some hot dancers."

"I'm seething," said Matthew. "I'm turning green, can you see me?"

"Hm." Frankie pretended to examine his face. "No."

"Maybe just a little, around the gills?"

"Nothing."

"All right. I can't work myself up about the chess guys. Peter-Porter what's-his-name better be glad he went to bed early, though." Matthew laughed.

"Welsch," said Frankie. "Porter Welsch."

Frankie had never before thought to ask Matthew what he was doing on the nights he cut out of the library at nine to "go meet Alpha," or on the evenings she didn't see him at all.

But in the days after that canceled date and the meeting in the catwalks, she followed him.

She found herself to be a talented tail—as if her years of meek inconsequentiality had trained her. She remembered what if felt like to be invisible—and she felt as if she could will herself back to that invisibility and follow Matthew and his friends quite easily, just by becoming the girl they'd never noticed. (If, in fact, they had honestly never noticed her.) In any case, she was swift. She was silent. She had an unerring sense of direction and a sharp intuition. And she owned a black coat and dark gloves, which didn't hurt.

The Bassets met fairly often in the days before Halloween. Frankie witnessed a meeting down by the pond Sunday night and a small meeting Tuesday after lunch, when she trailed Dean, Callum, Matthew, and Alpha back to a library study carrel, where they conferred alone for fifteen minutes. She couldn't hear what they were saying; but as they headed out through the stacks, they mentioned another conference Tuesday night in the theater.

What she heard at the meetings was relatively uneventful. The Bassets chanted the oath and drank beer or soda and ate chips.

Atop the crown of Alabaster,
Bind it tight with sticking plaster.
Look to the west, boys;
Look to the books, men!
History is our guide!
Keep the secrets, tunnel under,
Climb the heights, our pack defend.
The Basset is a hardy beast,
We vow our loyalty to the end.

They bickered over what to do on Halloween, but more often than not, talk degenerated into stuff about girls, sports, and other matters of a decidedly unsecret nature. Callum couldn't get anywhere with Gidget. The lacrosse team was having an awesome year. The seniors were applying to colleges.

However, Frankie was not confused. She understood exactly what was going on, because the purpose of the Loyal Order was connection. Bonding. Exclusivity. Maleness.

And even though Frankie found the meetings disorganized and their Halloween ideas dumb, she wanted to be part of it. They had such a large part of Matthew's heart, and Matthew had them.

They had such loyalty and joy.

And because of her sex, because of her age, because (perhaps) of her religion and her feminism, she could sit at their table every day and she would never, never, ever get in.

Frankie had fallen in love not only with Matthew but with his group of friends. And she knew they didn't rate her as anyone important.

Sure, they liked Frankie fine, found her attractive and didn't seem to mind her hanging around; but if Matthew had dumped her, none of them would ever have given Frankie a second glance. None of them.

It was a closed door.

Only—

The oath. They chanted it because they'd always chanted it, because even to teenage boys who might never publicly admit it, the act of chanting together creates a bond. But she could tell that few of them had ever listened to the actual words.

Bind it tight with sticking plaster. When Hank

Sutton had refused to tell Frankie about *The Disreputable History*, Dr. Montague had said, "Bind it tight with sticking plaster," and Senior had added, "Look to the west, boys!" As if the oath were the answer to the question she had asked: Where do you keep this history?

The oath was a puzzle. It would tell her where the history was.

And none of the current members of the Order seemed to even know it existed.

The second time Frankie heard the oath, as she hid in the trees on Sunday, listening to them toss pennies into the pond and discuss Callum's chances with the still-elusive Gidget, she wrote down the words. And that night she sat in bed with a flashlight, making notes.

The crown of Alabaster. What is this? Flagpole? Main building? New gym? Some person, famous alum?

Bind it tight—what is *it*, the thing being bound? The history itself?

Sticking plaster—Google says adhesive tape.

Look to the west. West from where? From the crown of Alabaster? or more metaphorical, meaning look to the West, look out to the expansion, gold rush, etc.

Look to the books. General exhortation to

excellence? Study hard? Or is it literal—look to the books, meaning toward the library? They do have meetings in the library.

History is our guide. Probably just that there's a history of the Bassets, hidden somewhere, that they should use as a guide. But possibly the history building?

Keep the secrets. Self-explanatory.

Tunnel under. Do basset hounds make tunnels? Google. Okay. They don't. So what tunneling does this mean? Tunneling under what?

Back to crown of Alabaster: New arts complex? Catwalks over theater? No. Widow's walk?

Climb the heights. Just metaphorical striving for excellence/power, etc.? Or something else. Heights of what?

Our pack defend. Obvious.

Hardy beast, etc. Obvious.

The Crown of Alabaster

◉

THE NEXT DAY, Frankie cut all her classes.

The details of her many false moves and fruitless investigations are boring, but suffice it to say she spent two hours in the domed top floor of the library searching for a hidden door, seven minutes examining the flagpole, fifteen minutes breaking into the storage room where extra flags were kept, and forty-two minutes searching that room. She vetoed the new gym and the arts complex as possible "crowns" because she was guessing the oath of the Loyal Order had been written years and years ago—long before even Senior was a Basset, and certainly before the new buildings were constructed. She spent a significant portion of her time before lunch navigating the catwalks in the old theater, silently observing the drama classes taking place on the stage below. She searched for items wrapped in sticky tape, books, or maps. She looked to the west, but all she could see were draperies and light-ing equipment.

Of course, it did occur to her to call Senior and ask him. He obviously knew exactly what the oath meant. Only—Frankie knew her father held his memberships close. He'd vowed his loyalty to the Order of the Basset Hounds, and he would never reveal their secrets, no matter how trivial or silly they might be. Not even to his own daughter. That had been clear at the steak house.

So Frankie called Zada instead, as she headed out of the old theater and over to the widow's walk.

"I'm on Telegraph at a coffeehouse and I'm wait-ing for someone, so I don't have much time," said Zada. "What's up?"

"Hi, Zada."

"Hi, you. How come you're calling me? You never call me in the middle of the day."

"You know that Basset thing Senior sometimes talks about? Like a club he was in at Alabaster?"

"The Basset Hounds. Yeah."

"What else do you know about them?"

"He never gives any details. It was like a secret society. There were rumors about it when I was at school, like it was a group of guys who did mysterious

199

things late at night. But I never saw much evidence."

"Well, it exists. I know people in it."

"Are you joining the Basset Hounds?" Zada was incredulous. "What do they do?"

"I can't join. It's all guys, all seniors."

"Matthew, right? Is he telling you all their Basset Houndy secrets? I'm dying to know. We could drive Senior crazy if you came home knowing all about his precious society."

"Matthew's not telling me," said Frankie. "That's just it. I kind of found out behind his back."

"So. What did you find out? I've always suspected Senior was up to some stuff he won't tell us about for fear of being a bad role model."

"So far it's not that much. Mainly bonding. Drinking beer or meeting in secret places, like up on the catwalks or in a library carrel. I think they pull pranks every now and then. They painted the Guppy on Halloween two years ago."

Zada giggled. "Oh, that was funny."

"Yeah. It's—Zada, you don't remember anything more that Senior said? Anything about a history they wrote that was hidden away somewhere?"

"No. Please. I do everything I can to prevent him from talking to me about his days at Alabaster. The man is seriously boring."

Frankie laughed. "We do have a very boring dad."

"Why are you asking about the Bassets, Frankie? You already know way more than I do."

It was difficult to explain. "They won't let me in," Frankie finally said.

"Did you ask?"

"You have to be tapped."

"What if you just asked? I bet Matthew would help you get in."

"I already told you, it's for senior guys. A certain kind of senior guy."

"And all they do is drink beer and paint statues? Why would you even want to bother?"

"That's what Trish would say, but you're missing the point."

"Oh, Frankie, my friend is walking through the door right now. So make it quick. What's the point, then?"

"Power, I guess."

"What?"

"Like Senior's always saying: It's how the world works. People form these bonds at school."

"Oh, give me a break, Frankie. *Hi, Saffron, just a minute, I'm on with my sister and she's stressing about some boy thing.* Are you seriously going to tell me you buy into the patriarchal notion that power is localized in institutions created years and years ago by people who were overly proud of themselves for having the male set of genitalia, and most of whom are either dead or drooling over themselves in nursing homes by this point?"

"Well—"

"Please, that is so antiquated. The institutions of male supremacy only have real power over you if you buy into that notion. Go found your own club and tell them *they* can't join. Or better yet, drop the idea of clubs altogether because they're exclusionary, and embrace some other, more flexible way of connecting with people."

"But, Zada." Frankie wanted to explain about the door being closed, about wanting to push through the door, about wanting not to feel small and second-best at the table. But Zada cut her off.

"Don't stress over this, Frankie. It's okay if Matthew's in some dumb drinking club that you're not in. Just let him be in it and go do your own thing."

"All right."

"Now take a deep breath and go back to your class. Okay, Bunny Rabbit? Because I know you're missing class."

"It's lunch already."

"Okay, then. I'm hanging up now. Bye."

Zada was gone.

Alabaster Preparatory School had begun some 120 years

ago on a piece of land that had been subsequently developed into the large, rambling campus where Frankie went to school. At its inception, however, there had been only two buildings: the semi-renovated Founder's Hall (English department) and Founder's House, a large, white, Victorian-style house where the founder himself had lived, now a small museum of minor local interest. It housed a collection of first-edition novels, plus a bunch of nice china and some antiques.

At the top of Founder's House was a widow's walk, even though Alabaster was nowhere near the ocean. Visitors could get there by mounting a steep staircase from the third-floor hall. Once up, they'd find a square, railed observation platform on the roof that allowed a 360-degree view of the campus. Against the north railing was a bronze map of Alabaster, annotated with tidbits of information about various buildings.

At the door to Founder's House sat a docent, someone equipped to hand out pamphlets and point the way to the bathroom. Frankie smiled at him, flashed her student ID, and made a show of walking quietly through the ground floor of the house, gazing at first editions. As soon as she could, however, she scurried to the top floor, down the hall, and began climbing the stairs to the widow's walk.

If this is the crown, Frankie thought as she went up, then I should look to the west and see if I can see anything that gives a clue as to where the history is hidden. Also, look to the books—the dome of the library.

She pushed open the door and stopped for a moment, blinking in the sun.

Standing in front of her was Alpha Tesorieri. Looking west.

Look to the West, Boys

◉

ALPHA JUMPED when he saw her, but soon smiled. "Hello."

"Hey. I didn't expect to see you here."

"I didn't expect you, either."

Why was he here? He must have figured out the oath.

If he didn't know there was a history, he was at least looking for *something* here on the crown.

If this *was* the crown.

It must be.

Could Alpha have any clue that Frankie was here because of the Basset Hound oath?

No.

Yes.

Maybe. It was a stretch, but maybe.

"Such a coincidence," Frankie said, wandering over to gaze at the map. The library was northwestish from Founder's House, which didn't help much. The history building—worth a try—was to the south.

"What brings you up?" asked Alpha.

Frankie thought, I've got to keep him from looking west. Keep him from figuring anything more out.

"It's such a pretty day," Alpha continued, when she didn't answer. "I came to look at the view. Fall is the best season. Hey, do you see that tree that's completely purple?"

"Where?"

He pointed it out. "That shouldn't even be a color that's in nature. It doesn't look real. Don't you love it?"

It was a beautiful tree. "It's like it doesn't know it's supposed to be brown. No one told it. So it's busted out with the purple," Frankie said.

"Exactly," said Alpha. "Now I'll ask you again. What brings you up?"

"I have a project for my Cities class," Frankie lied. "We have to come here and make observations about the layout of Alabaster—the way the design of the school enforces or encourages particular ideologies and behaviors." She was astonished at how easy it was to invent a plausible answer.

"Interesting," said Alpha, his eyes flitting west again.

What did he see there? There was the library, slightly north, and directly west the earth sciences building. Beyond that the old theater, and then the woods.

Frankie walked to the southern railing, searching for something to distract him. "There's a path across the quad that's worn by people's feet, do you see? Going diagonally from the main building to the door of the caf. No one wants to stay on the paths, even though it's not that much quicker to walk on the grass."

Alpha walked over and looked down. "It goes right by the 'Keep Off the Grass' sign, too."

"No one seems to worry about getting caught."

Alpha laughed. His arm was touching hers as they leaned on the railing. "I wouldn't worry. That's the sort of thing where if you get caught, nothing happens," he said. "A security guard scolds you. That's it. You're not going to get expelled."

"But it's such a pointless little rebellion," objected Frankie. "'Ooh, I'm gonna walk on the grass when the signs tell me not to! Look at me.' When those same people would never break any other rules. Not any that would matter."

"It feels good to be disobedient, don't you think?" asked Alpha. He leaned his weight ever so slightly harder against her arm, and Frankie could smell cigarette smoke and a wisp of apple.

She didn't quite want to pull away, but she did.

"It feels good to off-road across the quad," Alpha continued, as if nothing had just happened.

"It's hardly off-roading," she said. But inside she thought: Was he flirting with me? Did I imagine it?

"Yeah," Alpha said, "but that's exactly what those car salesmen are selling when they sell those SUV off-roaders. The *idea* of off-roading. No one's seriously driving their van up a mountaintop. They just want to be the kind of guys who *would* drive up there. Guys who don't stay on the path."

He was arguing just like he did with his friends in the caf. Like he liked her. Like he respected what she was going to say next.

He hadn't been flirting with her. "You're saying everyone likes to think of himself as a guy who doesn't stay on the path?" Frankie asked.

"Sure. Who wants to be the guy on the path?"

Frankie didn't—but she didn't want to be the guy whose idea of off-roading was an SUV purchase or a shortcut across the grass, either. "If everyone's off the path," she wondered, "then isn't it an illusion? Like they all think they're nocuous rebels, but really they just spent a lot on the same car all their neighbors spent a lot on?"

Alpha laughed. "Nocuous? Like the positive of innocuous? That's funny."

We haven't been alone together since that day on the beach, Frankie thought, looking into his wide face as it crinkled in amusement. I wonder if he's remembering it, too. But instead she said, "Yeah. It's the same type of people who convince themselves they're cool by walking across the quad, when actually they're treading the exact same path half the student body treads every day, and they're only breaking a rule the school obviously doesn't care about enforcing."

"You have a point," conceded Alpha. "But doesn't that 'Keep Off the Grass' sign bother you? Doesn't it make you want to walk on the grass?"

"No."

"Doesn't it annoy you to go all the way down to the corner there and then make a left turn to get to the caf, when you could get there faster across the quad, because some landscape guy, like, a hundred years ago decided that was how the path should go?"

"I think there are bigger things to rebel against," said Frankie. "If I want to be off-roading, I should be doing some major and serious off-roading. Why waste my off-roading energies on the dumb quadrangle?"

"Yeah, but with serious off-roading you risk actually getting in trouble," said Alpha.

"Did you really run a cockfight on the Lower East Side?" Frankie asked him. She had always been curious, and she wanted to come away from this encounter understanding something more about Alpha than she had before.

He looked at her, surprised. "That's for me to know," he answered, smiling.

"No, really—did you?"

"I'm not going to corrupt you with tales of my bad behavior. Look." He pointed down. "There's your boyfriend."

Sure enough. Matthew was standing in front of Founder's House, gazing up at them.

Frankie and Alpha met Matthew on the steps out front. "My two favorite people," Matthew said, looking genuinely pleased to see them. "I was practically alone at lunch."

"You were not." Alpha shook his head.

"Well, except for Dean and Callum and Steve and Tristan," said Matthew. "But I missed you. Callum and I built a desert island habitat using forks, mashed potatoes, and banana skins."

"I forgot my books," Frankie remembered, and ran back into the Founder's House foyer to collect her bag. While she was in there, she heard Alpha saying to Matthew: "Dog, she showed up on the widow's walk. Why would she show up on the widow's walk?"

"Don't be paranoid. She would never mess with us," said Matthew. "And besides, she doesn't even know anything about anything. I promise you, she's harmless."

"I'm not sure."

"Be sure. I know her way better than you do," said Matthew.

"I didn't find jack up there," said Alpha. "But it's worth going back. Every other possibility has turned out dead."

Frankie joined them, and they escorted her to her sixth-period class.

Alpha insisted they walk diagonally across the quad.

BIND IT TIGHT WITH
STICKING PLASTER

TRISH'S BOYFRIEND ARTIE was an AVT guy. This meant he was one of the students who knew how to work the classroom DVD players, hook the teachers' laptops up to projectors, and so on.

Artie had keys.

In a small, darkened room of Founder's House, there ran a short film of Alabaster students in 1938 playing various sports, raising flags, and standing proudly in front of the Guppy. Artie had been in there to fix the projector more than once.

Which meant that Artie had keys to Founder's House.

The building would close by five p.m.—before anyone was out of sports practice, so Alpha couldn't return until ten a.m. the following day, if he could get himself excused from class somehow, and not until lunch, otherwise. To be sure of beating him, though, Frankie had to get in there before the place opened the next morning.

Directly after modern dance, she called in a favor from Trish. "I just need them for twenty-four hours, the sooner starting, the better," she said as they stood by their lockers peeling off sweat-soaked leotards.

"What are you up to?" Trish narrowed her eyes as she wrapped a towel around herself and headed for the shower.

Frankie followed, her voice low. "Nothing. Something. I won't steal anything."

"You could get suspended for this, you know that?"

Frankie nodded.

"I mean, it's one thing to be out on the golf course after curfew, but letting yourself into locked buildings full of valuable china and whatever—the administration is gonna take that seriously."

"No one will see me," promised Frankie. "I'll be totally petuous."

"I don't know," said Trish. "I feel like they see everything."

"Trust me," said Frankie. "You can be completely turbed."

"You're not even talking normal." Trish closed the curtain on the shower stall and turned on the water. She didn't speak for a few minutes. Frankie stood under the spray in the next stall over, knowing that her thoughts had crossed some kind of line.

If she were normal, she would be worried about her geometry test and whether she'd get a good part in the midwinter dance show and whether Zada was okay off in California with degenerate Berkeley students and whether Matthew loved her like she loved him.

But nothing seemed important except getting herself back on that roof.

Matthew had called her harmless. Harmless. And being with him made Frankie feel squashed into a box—a box where she was expected to be sweet and sensitive (but not oversensitive); a box for young and pretty girls who were not as bright or powerful as their boyfriends. A box for people who were not forces to be reckoned with.

Frankie wanted to be a force.

"Okay," said Trish, turning off the water and heading back toward her locker.

"You'll do it?"

"I said, okay."

"Thank you," said Frankie, shutting off her own shower and following, wrapping a towel around her as she went. "I am so mayed."

"What?"

"Mayed."

Trish sighed. "From dismayed?"

"Exactly."

"You're going crazy. You do know that, right?"

"Yah. Probably."

Trish went with Artie to "study" in his dorm room after dinner, and came back with the AVT keys in her pocket. "He's gonna miss them by Wednesday afternoon, for sure," she told Frankie, handing them over. "So do whatever your creepy business is and get them back to me before then. He has to work the movie projector for the senior cinema elective."

"Got it. Thanks."

"And don't copy them."

"I won't," lied Frankie. "I would never."

The keys were on a large ring, twenty-five all together, but Frankie got lucky. The fourth one she tried fit the lock. No alarm system. She had a small flashlight on her, but she kept it off, feeling her way up three flights of stairs and onto the roof.

She stood at the west railing of the widow's walk, staring out. The library was there, just to the north, but what was she to see? Was there some secret in the buildings?

Or was whatever the chant referred to long gone? The campus had developed and changed since the oath was written, probably fifty years ago.

It sounded like the history was bound with tape. But how could anything be bound with tape that she could see from up here?

Frankie flicked her flashlight on briefly and walked over to the north railing to look at the bronze map. It was dated 1947, and didn't include the new gymnasium, the arts complex, or the addition to the science building.

Look to the west, boys. On impulse, Frankie dropped to her knees and felt underneath the map. The underside was smooth, unlike the raised surface, and she ran her fingers over the cool west edge.

Nothing.

Look to the books, men! She ran her hands up and down the underside methodically, and there, underneath the tiny raised dome of the library, stuck to bronze with duct tape, was a small package.

It took most of twenty minutes to loosen the ancient silver tape enough to release it. When she did, Frankie flipped on her flashlight and shined it on the object in her lap. Wrapped in three layers of paper bags was a small leather-bound notebook.

HISTORY

◉

he *Disreputable History of the Loyal Order of the Basset Hounds* is filled with the minuscule print of schoolboys beginning in 1951. On the inside of the first page is a surprisingly competent painting of a basset hound, done in watercolor. The basset looks serious and ridiculous, simultaneously.

Herein are tales of the adventures of Bassets from the beginning of the Loyal Order, transcripted for use of future generations. Let history be your guide, oh hounds of the future!
We, the undersigned, do formally commit ourselves to acts of disreputability, ridiculousness, and anarchy, reserving the possibility that we will also commit acts

of indecency and illegality, should the
occasions call for it.

The Basset kings had recorded the activities of the club from its '51 founding until—Frankie flipped forward—1975. That year, as was clear from the erratic handwriting as well as the prose, the primary activity of the Bassets (including one future president of the United States) was the smoking of marijuana. And because there was now this detailed record of the Loyal Order's most illegal activity yet—the bags of "grass" and the "doobies" they smoked on the widow's walk late at night on weekends—the Basset king that year (one Hank Sutton) insisted that a poetic Basset named Franklin Banks write a poem that simultaneously sang the praises of the Loyal Order and which would indicate for future members the top-secret hiding place of the *Disreputable History*, so that it wouldn't be in danger of falling into the wrong hands over summer vacation.

Banks wrote the poem after inhaling, and that's why it had come out as obscure as it had. He'd also set it to music, strumming on a guitar late at night in his dorm room. The next day he taught it to all the Bassets, including the future kings, and shortly thereafter, he and Sutton graduated—without ever telling the younger boys where they'd hid the History.

"Our song will reach down through the ages," Sutton wrote, "and this record of our misdeeds and adventures will be unearthed when grass is legal and no harm can come to our reputations."

Those younger Bassets had been too dumb to find the history, Frankie guessed. Probably they searched, but without luck. Years passed, and no one found it— and it was not long before none of them knew there had ever been a history at all. The oath had become nothing but an oath.

The book had been lost for more than thirty years.

And her father used to smoke pot with that old Sutton guy.

Frankie flipped back to the beginning.

"September 30, 1951," wrote the king who signed his posts Connelly. "The first and foremost goal of the Loyal Order of the Basset Hounds is to acquire the Guppy."

And then, in an entry written two weeks later:

The Guppy has been seized. Bassets Kennedy and Hardewick dressed in aprons and carried a large flower-delivery box. Skipping chapel (a time when the proverbial coast was guaranteed clear) they approached the piscine statue unobserved and loosened it from its moorings with wrenches and a bobby pin

Kennedy had his sister send him in a package. Hardewick and Kennedy enclosed the Guppy in the box and loaded it into Hardewick's car. The Guppy now resides in the basement of the Hardewick house in Williamstown.

Administration furious. Students protesting, demanding return of Guppy for Alabaster morale and good fellowship. Local paper covers event.

Basset Sheffield's genius idea put into execution: we sent a note to the administration promising return of the Guppy in exchange for leniency and ten boxes of Mars bars. Administration agreed. Mars bars were delivered to a specified location and a flower box was returned to the headmaster's office containing ... an actual guppy.

(We are hereby regretful that the life of an innocent guppy was taken as a result of our mission, and resolve not to harm any more animals in the pursuit of our misdeeds.)

Anyway, administration absolutely livid. Actual stone Guppy to be returned the day after graduation so long as Hardewick's mom doesn't find it in her basement. Tee-hee.

In 1968, the Order erected a small tent on the central quad, outside of which was a sign: "Do Not Enter."

Inside was nothing at all. The rather esoteric Basset king that year had simply wanted to see if people would disobey the sign, given that there was no apparent reason for the prohibition. Few of them did.

That same year they posted an official-looking list of rules in the caf—some of which were reasonable ("Do not cut in line; do not take two entrees") and one of which read "Please walk only on the black tiles." For the first few hours, the History reported, many students did in fact attempt to walk only on the black squares of the checkerboard floor.

Other years the pranks had been more traditional: Bassets had toilet-papered the headmaster's car, hung underpants from flagpoles, put Jell-O in the toilets, and booby-trapped the doors of unwitting teachers.

Some years, the entries were packed with anecdotes, while others consisted of the barest sketches. Most years, the members pledged eternal loyalty to one another in writing, promising to "back each other through and through" and "never to forget, never to reveal."

What struck Frankie most, as she read, was the sense of togetherness. The king usually wrote most of the entries, but Bassets edited each other's writing, scribbled in comments, and took turns telling stories as well. They planned to know one another when they were ancient and gray—"when we're doddering around with canes and have forgotten the names of our wives, we will still be Bassets, and still be young in our hearts," wrote one rhapsodic boy in 1957.

The notebook was tattered, and on every fragile page Frankie could feel the fundamental connection between the boys. They were going through life together—whether the pranks they pulled were dumb or brilliant.

She was going through life with no one.

At the back of the notebook, a key was attached to the inside of the jacket with sticky tape. Underneath it was written in the cramped schoolboy script of Connelly: Hazelton, sub-16.

Hazelton was the library.

English Muffins

ON WEDNESDAY before Halloween, Elena Tesorieri demanded Alpha leave school for several days. It was a manufactured crisis. Elena couldn't bear the empty penthouse and insisted Alpha accompany her *and her mother* to a yoga retreat in the Berkshires. She said it would be good for him, and she missed her son, and the retreat was necessary to her mental health—but her own mother would drive her batty if Alpha wasn't there to act as buffer.

He had classes, papers due, secret-society pranks to orchestrate—Elena didn't care. To the Berkshires he would go, for four days over Halloween.

An hour before his departure, Alpha held court at lunch in the caf. "Can you picture me?" he asked. "I'm like the most inflexible man alive. There will be all these fifty-year-old women wearing hot pants and squeezing themselves into pretzel shapes and then there will be me. Just reaching for my toes like they're China. 'Hello, there! You're so far away, I can't get to you! Can you even hear me?'"

"I think some meditation could be good for you," said Elizabeth.

"What? You think I'm high-strung?" Alpha laughed and dunked a french fry into his soda. "I'm the guy who's blowing off the calculus test and the Euro history paper, not to mention the Harvard early-action application I am supposed to be finishing, all to go do stretchy exercises in the woods."

"I'm just saying. It wouldn't hurt you to mellow out."

"You'll see. I'm gonna come back here with like ultra yoga man vibrations coming out of my pores. Those yoga guys are very sexy. You'll be completely unable to resist my charms."

Elizabeth snorted.

Frankie thought: Alpha and Elizabeth are having sex. Is Matthew upset that he and I aren't having sex?

And then she thought: He's leaving school. Alpha is leaving school.

"You gonna call in about the Halloween thing?" Callum asked.

"Shut up. We're in the caf," snapped Alpha.

"Did you have too much coffee?" Callum complained. "Sheesh, you're like trip-wired."

"No," said Alpha, answering the original question. "I can't call in. No cell phones, no Internet. This yoga place is old-school."

And Frankie thought: He won't even be able to call anyone. Incommunicado for four days.

"Well, what are we doing?" Callum persisted.

"Later," said Matthew, looking at his food. "You have a big mouth, you know that?"

Callum laughed. "I know. Literally. Frankie, you wanna see me fit three English muffins in my big mouth? I seriously can."

Dean nodded. "He can. It is a truly vile sight."

"Sure," said Frankie, handing over the two halves of a toasted English that were sitting on her tray. "You want butter?"

And inside, she thought: Four days. That's an opening if I ever saw one.

But for what? An opening for what?

"Nah," said Callum. "Butter is cheating. It greases them up. The pure accomplishment must be done without the aid of butter."

"At the yoga place," said Alpha, tossing Callum his English muffins, "they teach you to put four in your mouth at once. Every morning, every single person there practices at breakfast. They put in all four, and anyone who chews it all and swallows without gagging gets a prize."

"He is so full of it," sighed Elizabeth.

"What's the prize?" asked Matthew.

"Oh, um. Let's see, the prize is some kind of certificate of English muffin enlightenment, and once you have eight of them you get a medal that proves you are Master of the Muffin. I'm serious. All the yoga teachers can do six muffins. They do six muffins every morning as a matter of course."

Callum had wedged the three muffins into his mouth and was grunting and pointing to his face.

"Very good," said Frankie.

Thinking: An opening for the Halloween prank, that's what.

"It's nothing!" cried Alpha. "Haven't you been listening to me? When I get back from yogaland, I am going to out-muffin his dumb jock self. You wait and see."

Joke as he might—and all Alpha's powers of self-aggrandizement in the guise of amusing self-deprecation were called into play here—the alpha male had been effectively and efficiently (though temporarily) emasculated by his mommy.

Frankie felt a glow of schadenfreude, which quickly changed into excitement. She ducked out of lunch early and took Artie's keys to the hardware store, where she made copies of each and every one. Then she slid into sixth period fifteen minutes late, dropping the keys into Trish's backpack with an apologetic smile, just in time for Artie to spend seventh period showing films to the senior cinema elective.

In between classes, Frankie opened her laptop, went online, and opened a Gmail account.

Screen name: THEALPHADOG.

What she planned to do with this e-mail account during Alpha's absence was not yet clear to Frankie. Something, though.

Something big.

Something Halloween.

She had to sort it out, fast.

At nine twenty p.m. that evening, as she took off her own plain cotton bra and pulled on her pajama top, Frankie noticed Trish's blue lace underwire lying on the floor of their dorm room.

She thought: That's a silly bra.

And then she thought: But it's cute.

It just seems so funny to dress up your boobs. Like when no one is going to see them. Or even if someone is. It seems so undignified to deck out your private bits in flashy bits of lace you'd never wear on the outside of your clothes in a million years.

And then she thought: Boobs.

Boobs are just inherently undignified.

These are what I've got that keeps me out of the Loyal Order. Yes, it's my chromosomes, and maybe other things, too, but for a symbol of the difference between me and those boys—I could do worse than boobs. Or a bra.

Just then someone knocked. Frankie pulled on her bathrobe and answered. It was Artie, with two of his friends from AVT, Charles and John. They were a riot of sparkle, color, and ridiculous amounts of lipstick. All three of them were dressed in drag.

"Hey, is Trish here?" Artie said, giggling. "We're having a dress rehearsal for Halloween. I need her advice."

"She's in Mabel's room cramming for the geography test," said Frankie, stepping out in the hall to admire them. "Aren't co-study hours nearly over? They're gonna kick you guys out of here any second."

"Oh, we've got ten minutes," said Artie. "What do you think? How do we look?"

He twirled, showing himself off. He wore patent-leather high heels, bold stripes of blush across his cheekbones, and a purple taffeta party dress.

"What are you supposed to be?" Frankie asked.

"What do you mean?"

"What are you dressed up as? Like, are you a singing group or something?"

"No, no. Just girls," Artie answered. "Right?" He turned to his friends, who nodded. "Just girls."

Do girls really look like that to them? wondered Frankie. Because she felt like she herself was the furthest thing from this shiny, fluffy, lipsticky creature in front of her, this Artie in drag. "Good luck with that."

"Can I ask you something?" Charles said.

"Sure."

"Do we need to shave our legs? I'm trying to avoid that by wearing black hose."

"You don't have to," Frankie told him. "I hardly think you're going for realism here." He was wearing a silver miniskirt and platform heels. He was six foot one.

"Oh yes I am!" he cried. "I don't want to have my leg hairs showing!"

"Then you have to shave, Charles," said Artie dryly. "I told you already."

"He wants to see if Trish will lend him one of her bras," piped up John, dressed in a pink strapless prom dress.

"I got this one from Charlie's sister," explained Artie. "But it's only an A-cup. I want to have a little more impact."

"You can ask her," Frankie said. "Mabel's in room 209."

"Or could he have one of yours?" John wondered.

229

"I dulge that," said Frankie. "My underwear is not going out on loan."

"Dulge?" Artie squinted at her.

"Neglected positive of indulge. I'm not indulging that idea of yours. I'm dulging it. No bra."

"Come on," pleaded John. "Just till Halloween."

"Shut up!" said Artie. "She doesn't have to. I can get one from Trish."

"If you put a shrug on over those outfits," said Frankie, "you won't have to shave your armpits."

"Oh no! I forgot about armpits!" cried John.

"I forgot about armpits, too!" moaned Charles, whose shirt was nothing more than a camisole. "What's a shrug?"

"Like a minisweater," Frankie told him.

"There are so many girl-things we don't know!" cried Charles. "I'm so glad we did a dress rehearsal. This would have been a disaster otherwise."

"Come on, ladies," said Artie. "We have to go to 209 and find me a bra."

"And a shrug," said John.

"Two shrugs," said Charles. "I'm still going to see if I can get through this whole night without shaving anything. Bye, Frankie!"

Frankie watched them totter on unsteady heels down to Mabel's room. Then she shut the door behind her and flipped open her laptop.

She was very, very gruntled.

She had her plan. It was full and complete, down to nearly every detail. It had formed itself in the back of her head while Artie and the boys were talking about their costumes, and waited, poised, to flood itself into her mind the moment they departed.

She started by Googling the word *parachute*.

How to Get Through
a Closed Door

◉

You will recall that Frankie had been researching and writing early drafts of her Cities, Art, and Protest paper on the San Francisco Suicide Club and the Cacophony Society. SantaCon? The Brides of March? Clowns on a Bus? You remember.

After Frankie opened the Gmail account, she wrote an initial draft of the following section, which is useful for a full understanding of what happened next:

The upperclassmen at the California Institute of Technology skip school each year for a day and depart campus. The tradition is called "Ditch Day," and it has morphed from a simple prank against the university administration into a complicated back-and-forth. Now, those who traditionally were *committing* the prank (the upperclassmen, by skipping) have become those who are *pranked against*.

It all began when, with the seniors gone, the underclassmen started breaking into their rooms and booby-trapping their closets, moving the furniture around, emptying the rooms entirely (Steinberg, *If at All Possible, Involve a Cow: The Book of College Pranks*). So while the upperclassmen were asserting power over the *university*, the underclassmen asserted power over the upper.

But the upperclassmen fought back. They began to blockade their doors. It being Caltech, they quickly gave up blocking them with furniture and began "stacking" them with cement and huge pieces of metal. They booby-trapped the doors with sand and shaving cream. The underclassmen retaliated by using chain saws, bolt cutters, and jackhammers.

They got into the rooms so often that the seniors resorted to what Neil Steinberg calls the "finesse stack"—which challenges the underclassmen to solve a problem in the hallway before they can get into the room. It works on the honor system. The door is left open, and the students must reassemble an engine, decode seemingly random notes played by a synthesizer, or solve some other extremely complicated puzzle that has no doubt taken the upperclassman (or woman) many weeks to create.

A later development was the upperclassmen's invention of the "honor stack," which asks the younger students to go out and "Humiliate themselves in a variety of creative ways, tied together under an underlying plot or scenario" (Steinberg 150). They've got to run naked through campus, buy a house, or steal the athletic director's car.

Steinberg sees this struggle as symmetrical: "the underclassmen wanting in, the seniors wanting to keep them out" (147). But I think the most interesting thing about Ditch Day is the way the older students went from pranking authority by skipping school to *being* the authority that was pranked by the younger ones. Then the younger ones would often end up counterpranked by the stacks the seniors had created.

The administration was forgotten along the way, until the time of the honor stack, when the seniors managed to get the younger students to do their antiadministration pranks *for* them. So the younger students, thinking they were sending up the seniors by gaining access to their rooms, were sending up the school itself by running nude, stealing cars, etc.

These pranks resemble the activities of the Suicide Club/Cacophony Society in that they take a symbol (a closed door, symbolizing privacy) and reinvent it. The closed door of a senior on Ditch Day symbolizes a challenge to the underclassman (or woman). It says, "Break through me" or "Outwit my owner."

Like Cacophonists, the Caltech students critique a time-honored institution (the university) by breaking its unwritten rules: you must wear clothes, you must honor your teachers, you must not attack fellow students' dorm rooms with chain saws.

Halloween

From: thealphadog@gmail.com
To: Porter Welsch [pw034@alabasterpreparatory.edu],
    Matthew Livingston [ml220@alabasterpreparatory.edu],
    Dean Enderby [de088@alabasterpeparatory.edu], Callum
    Whitstone [cw165@alabasterpreparatory.edu], and 7
    others . . .
Subject: Halloween. A Change of Plans.

Delete this as soon as you have memorized its contents.
Delete it from the server, too, you wiener dogs.
Got it? Good.

There is a change of plans for Halloween. The old plan is too
dumb. We need a prank on a large scale that will give the
proverbial F-U to the establishment and amuse our fellow
students to no end at the same time.

Each of you will be given separate instructions. Porter and Sam
will carry out the most dangerous parts of our mission, but this
operation is large-scale, and everyone has got to participate.

Some of you will have to snatch climbing equipment from the new gymnasium and be prepared to use it with a reasonable degree of skill.

Others will need to acquire a large quantity of ladies' under-clothing in amusing colors and patterns.

Still others will get the painting supplies from the basement of the old theater and make signs.

I have copies of all keys you'll need to complete your operation and have left them in an envelope under Livingston's door.

Oh, and I had a parachute FedEx'd to Enderby. So don't forget to check your mail, dog.

All other purchases should be made on the down low. Pay cash when you can and burn receipts. The necessary Internet purchase tasks have been distributed broadly among those of you who have bottomless credit cards.

Do not get caught.

The name of the mission? In the Ladies We Trust.
Over and out.

BEFORE THIS MISSIVE ARRIVED, the Basset Halloween plan had been tangled and disorganized. Members of the Loyal Order had disagreed as to what constituted something funny, and what was worth the trouble.

Dean had suggested they all dress as pirates—but was vetoed because pirates were so 2006, and besides, that wasn't a prank. Alpha had suggested painting the Guppy again, but Matthew shot that down as repetitive and too un-Bassetty. Sam had thought they should mow the shape of a giant basset hound into the grass of the quad, but it was argued that no one would know what it was and the lawn mower would make too much noise for a covert operation. Callum had argued for getting hold of thirty pumpkins, writing "Loyal Order of the Basset Hound" on them in Sharpie marker, and piling them in front of the door to the main building, obstructing entry. This would be done at five a.m. and would cause a great fuss when students first tried to go to class. But Alpha pooh-poohed this as dumb, while Matthew argued that facilities maintenance would remove the pumpkins before anyone even noticed them.

Finally it was agreed to fork the main quad (tines up) so that, viewed from above, the forks spelled out BEWARE THE BASSET. Sam and Porter were assigned to heist several jumbo boxes of plastic forks from the Front Porch. They and two less significant (but older) members of the Order were to wake at dawn and shove the forks into the grass, with Tristan and Callum overseeing from their dorm room, which had a window onto the quad.

Thursday morning, however, with Alpha departed for yogaland, all Bassets received the above e-mail, canceling the forking in favor of In the Ladies We Trust. In addition, each member of the Loyal Order received a private e-mail detailing his particular mission.

When Alabaster students awoke on Halloween morning, they found that the portraits of headmasters, literary figures, and board members on the walls of the main building, the science building, and the arts complex had been adorned with colorful brassieres in varying sizes. The founder himself wore a pink floral demi-cup, while the previous headmaster wore an enormous, navy blue support garment. No paintings were damaged in the process; each bra was affixed with clear plastic wire that tied around the back of the frame.

A small nymph statue near the pond wore a practical underwire in beige. The Guppy wore a hot-purple A-cup. Even the large tree in front of the library sported a bright red double-D from the sale bin at Victoria's Secret in town. The tag was still on, flapping gently in the October breeze.

The Hazelton library dome, which stood so proudly at the center of the campus, had been outfitted in a large, pale brown parachute—the kind designed for after-school activities and pee-wee gym class. In the center of the parachute, the dome's nub had been painted a rosy pink, and in case anyone missed the idea, from the front of the library hung a large, painted sign reading: IN THE LADIES WE TRUST.

On every campus notice board there was posted a note, a replica of which was soon delivered to every mailbox, both student and faculty.

REGARDING THE HALLOWEEN MASQUERADE

Even the dead among you will notice that our esteemed headmasters and board members— together with Mark Twain and the uninteresting scientists whose portraits hang in the sciences building—plus the tree in front of Hazelton,the Guppy, the nymph, even the dome itself, have finally, after years of watching the students' Halloween festivities with unabashed longing, dressed up for the holiday.

No longer must they stare sadly from the confines of their frames and architectural moorings. Now they can celebrate with the rest of us.

In the Ladies We Trust!
Happy Halloween.

At the bottom of the page, each notice was stamped with the rubber stamp that replicated the sealing-wax design on the golf course party invitations: a droopy-eared basset hound.

On Halloween morning, Frankie Landau-Banks, though she hadn't slept all night, had been in her bed from ten p.m. until shortly before breakfast.

When the portrait of the second Alabaster headmaster that hung in the lobby of the caf revealed himself in an electric-yellow padded bra, Frankie evinced sleepy-eyed, innocent surprise. She ate with Matthew and the other Bassets, all of whom looked pale and heavy-lidded, but among whom there was a distinct (though unspoken) atmosphere of triumph. Frankie wondered if any of them suspected her, half wanting them to know, and half hoping they'd never find out.

Over the course of the morning, no one spoke of anything else. As she left history class, Frankie caught up with Trish, Star, and Claudia.

"Why bras? That's what I wonder," Claudia was saying.

"Ooh, did you see the little pink demi-cup on the founder? That one is seriously cute," said Star. "I would totally wear that."

"I think it's like making fun of women," said Trish. "Like saying, look how stupid these old guys look wearing clothes that women wear every single day."

"I think it's more like objectification." Claudia

shook her head. "Like making the library dome into a giant boob so everyone could gawk at it. All these guys were making boob jokes in math this morning."

"Same thing," said Trish.

"I don't think so. One is objectification and one is denigration," said Claudia, ever the poser.

"Don't they go hand in hand?"

Frankie began wondering if she could make an inpea from *denigration*. *Nigration*: appreciation, upholding of value.

Maybe not.

"I just think it's funny!" Star was saying. "Maybe it's just saying, boobs are great! Because they are. I bet guys secretly wish they had them. Like they made the library into a giant goddess boob. Don't you think that could be it?"

"Couldn't it be pointing out how there are like, no women in any of the paintings on campus?" said Frankie. "Couldn't it be saying, 'Where are the women to fill out these bras?'"

"That's true, too!" cried Star, wiggling. "The nymph is the only girl."

"Did you know," Frankie went on as casually as she could, "that girls make up fifty-two percent of the student body here, but only about twenty percent of the upper administration?"

"Oh, wow. Now you're geeking out," said Star.

"Shut up." This from Trish.

"Well, like who knows that kind of thing?" Star asked. "It's so weird that she would know that."

Frankie ignored the insult. People were talking about what she'd done. She was happy just to be on their minds, whatever their opinions. "Ooh!" she cried, as if she'd just had a thought. "What if we consider that maybe all those bra-wearing founders and headmasters are trying to get in touch with their feminine side? They're dressing in drag, the way so many guys do on Halloween, because it's their only chance to experience any of the power of femininity?"

Claudia raised her eyebrows. "I don't think so."

"But the note said 'In the Ladies We Trust,'" persisted Frankie.

"I still think it's making fun of us," said Trish.

"Yay for the power of femininity!" cried Star.

The brassieres remained up until after lunch, when the maintenance team finished the usual morning tasks and began to untie them. The library boob (or "Library Lady" as we shall henceforth term it) remained up for most of the day, until workers equipped for scaling the roof could be located and hired. Mail delivery at noon, containing a copy of the aforementioned note for every member of the Alabaster community, started everyone talking all over again.

Matthew was positively buoyant, Frankie could tell—though he didn't say a word to her about the prank beyond feigning innocence and admiration.

Frankie was glad he was gruntled.

And she was angry that he wouldn't tell her why.

Both.

A Vamp

◉

WHEN ALPHA TESORIERI arrived back on campus Sunday evening, a last-minute meeting of the Loyal Order convened in the dark by the bridge at the edge of the pond. Frankie watched from the woods.

Stiff from four days of yoga, he rapidly consumed a large bag of potato chips while his dogs reported to him. Alpha's mastery of the situation was remarkable. Frankie had expected him to be furious at her hijacking of the Halloween prank. Expected to witness a thrashing and scolding of the dogs.

Eventually, she figured, he would suspect someone outside the pack and finally accuse her, angry but admiring her genius, acknowledging her as the superior mind.

But that is not what happened.

Though it was clear to Frankie that at first Alpha had no inkling of what had transpired at Alabaster over Halloween, he coolly and jovially lobbed back every conversational ball that came his way.

"Dog, I'm so glad you had us ditch the forks," said Sam. "I was not looking forward to that."

There was only the smallest beat before Alpha said, "It wasn't good enough."

"Brilliant," said Matthew. "I mean, really brilliant. You're an evil genius."

Alpha slapped him on the back. "That's my aim. Evil genius."

"Seriously," continued Matthew. "No one could have done better."

"Thanks. Dog, you and I should talk later."

"Where'd you find that parachute?" asked Callum.

"What?"

"The parachute."

"The Internet, where else?" answered Alpha.

"The e-mails were excellent," said Dean. "I don't know why we never thought of that, doing stuff through a mailing list."

"And how did you know where to buy the bras, dog?" asked Callum.

Alpha vamped. "Bras? You mean, bras?" He cupped his hands to his chest.

"Bras."

Alpha's voice betrayed none of the confusion he must have felt. "Hello. I have a girlfriend. But don't worry. I got the info out of her without her suspecting a thing."

"That letter was genius." Dean shook his head.

"You liked it?" He was poking for more information.

"Oh, yeah. 'In the Ladies We Trust!'"

"I did that before I left."

"How'd you get the gym key?" Sam wanted to know.

"Oh, I have my ways. My secret contacts."

"Porter nearly killed himself on that roof."

"Hey, Porter. Proving yourself worthy of the crown, excellent."

"Alpha," called Porter. "I have a question—"

"Dogs!" interrupted Alpha. "I have some serious caloric deprivation to make up for, and I haven't seen Elizabeth in four days. Can we cut this short now, if there's no agenda? I'll be in touch."

"Yes, oh Basset King."

Frankie sat on her sweater, some ten feet back from them in the dark. She didn't move until every one of them had wandered away.

She should have known this would happen. How had she not foreseen?

Alpha was taking credit.

Well, if he was going to play it that way, Frankie was going to raise the stakes.

THE SUBSEQUENT E-MAILS

From: thealphadog@gmail.com
To: Alessandro Tesorieri [at114@alabasterpreparatory.edu]

You cover well, Alessandro. One might almost believe you knew last night what had happened with the bras.
And the parachute.

> **From:** Alessandro Tesorieri [at114@alabasterpreparatory.edu]
> **To:** thealphadog@gmail.com
>
> WTF, you identity-snatching member of my own pack?

From: thealphadog@gmail.com
To: Alessandro Tesorieri [at114@alabasterpreparatory.edu]

I made you look good.

> **From:** Alessandro Tesorieri [at114@alabasterpreparatory.edu]
> **To:** thealphadog@gmail.com
>
> Bite me.

From: thealphadog@gmail.com
To: Alessandro Tesorieri [at114@alabasterpreparatory.edu]

My bite is worse than my bark.

> **From:** Alessandro Tesorieri [at114@alabasterpreparatory.edu]
> **To:** thealphadog@gmail.com
>
> What do you want?

From: thealphadog@gmail.com
To: Alessandro Tesorieri [at114@alabasterpreparatory.edu]

Wait and see.

> **From:** Alessandro Tesorieri [at114@alabasterpreparatory.edu]
> **To:** thealphadog@gmail.com
>
> Sam, you power-hungry weenie.

From: thealphadog@gmail.com
To: Alessandro Tesorieri [at114@alabasterpreparatory.edu]

I agree, Sam is a power-hungry weenie.
But I am not he.

> **From:** Alessandro Tesorieri [at114@alabasterpreparatory.edu]
> **To:** thealphadog@gmail.com
>
> Elizabeth, if this is you, that means you've been
> rummaging in my private papers, and that means:
> you are not my girlfriend anymore.

From: thealphadog@gmail.com
To: Alessandro Tesorieri [at114@alabasterpreparatory.edu]

The she-wolf didn't rummage your papers.

From: Alessandro Tesorieri [at114@alabasterpreparatory.edu]
To: thealphadog@gmail.com

You're like my doppelganger, is that it?

From: thealphadog@gmail.com
To: Alessandro Tesorieri [at114@alabasterpreparatory.edu]

Doppelganger: from the German word *doppel*, as in double; and *ganger*, as in walker. A double-walker.
It means a look-alike, Alessandro. Or an evil twin.
But me? I am invisible, and when you see me I look nothing like you.
So, no. I am not your doppelganger.

From: Alessandro Tesorieri [at114@alabasterpreparatory.edu]
To: thealphadog@gmail.com

What do you look like?

From: thealphadog@gmail.com
To: Alessandro Tesorieri [at114@alabasterpreparatory.edu]

I am better looking, Alessandro. And I have a cooler e-mail address.

From: Alessandro Tesorieri [at114@alabasterpreparatory.edu]
To: thealphadog@gmail.com

Don't call me Alessandro, or this could get ugly.

From: thealphadog@gmail.com
To: Alessandro Tesorieri [at114@alabasterpreparatory.edu]

Oh, then may I call you Alice?

From: Alessandro Tesorieri [at114@alabasterpreparatory.edu]
To: thealphadog@gmail.com

The Loyal Order has been around since the 1940s. The Basset kings are chosen by the kings the year before. It has always been done that way. Here's the protocol:
If you're not happy with what's going on at meetings, take it up with me or Livingston.
We'll listen to what you've got to say.

From: thealphadog@gmail.com
To: Alessandro Tesorieri [at114@alabasterpreparatory.edu]

You haven't even got your facts straight. The Loyal Order has been around since 1951, founded by Henry Connelly, Davie Kennedy, and Clayton Hardewick. Their first activity was the capturing of the Guppy and its subsequent entombment in Hardewick's mother's basement. They did not return it until graduation.
They wrote it all down in a book. *The Disreputable History of the Loyal Order of the Basset Hounds.*

From: Alessandro Tesorieri [at114@alabasterpreparatory.edu]
To: thealphadog@gmail.com

I know about the history already. Sam is a legacy. His dad told him, and Sam told me. As soon as we find it, we'll share it with the whole pack.

From: thealphadog@gmail.com
To: Alessandro Tesorieri [at114@alabasterpreparatory.edu]

I am looking at it right now.

From: Alessandro Tesorieri [at114@alabasterpreparatory.edu]
To: thealphadog@gmail.com

Whoever you are, that book is not your rightful property. It belongs to the Bassets. To the collective, not an individual member. Hasn't the Order served you well? Remember your vow of loyalty.

From: thealphadog@gmail.com
To: Alessandro Tesorieri [at114@alabasterpreparatory.edu]

If I took a vow of loyalty, it's slipped my mind.

> **From:** Alessandro Tesorieri [at114@alabasterpreparatory.edu]
> **To:** thealphadog@gmail.com
>
> Frankie Landau-Banks. Am I right?
> I knew you were up to no good on the widow's walk that day.

From: thealphadog@gmail.com
To: Alessandro Tesorieri [at114@alabasterpreparatory.edu]

You honestly think I'm Livingston's little girlfriend?
Don't insult me or you'll end up sorry. Try again, nimrod.
And if you're so upset, why not tell Livingston what's going on?

> **From:** Alessandro Tesorieri [at114@alabasterpreparatory.edu]
> **To:** thealphadog@gmail.com
>
> You know why I don't tell Livingston.

From: thealphadog@gmail.com
To: Alessandro Tesorieri [at114@alabasterpreparatory.edu]

Yes, I do know why.

> **From:** Alessandro Tesorieri [at114@alabasterpreparatory.edu]
> **To:** thealphadog@gmail.com
>
> Tell me you're not Livingston. Matthew would never do this.

From: thealphadog@gmail.com
To: Alessandro Tesorieri [at114@alabasterpreparatory.edu]

I'm not Livingston.

> **From:** Alessandro Tesorieri [at114@alabasterpreparatory.edu]
> **To:** thealphadog@gmail.com
>
> I want that book, you masquerading lunatic.

(Frankie did not reply to this one.)

> **From:** Alessandro Tesorieri [at114@alabasterpreparatory.edu]
> **To:** thealphadog@gmail.com
>
> Did you get my last e-mail? I want that book. Can we make a trade?

(No reply.)

> **From:** Alessandro Tesorieri [at114@alabasterpreparatory.edu]
> **To:** thealphadog@gmail.com
>
> What can I trade you for that book? There must be something you want, or you wouldn't have told me you have it.

(No reply.)

> **From:** Alessandro Tesorieri [at114@alabasterpreparatory.edu]
> **To:** thealphadog@gmail.com
>
> I want that book, psychopath.

(No reply.)

HOW MUCH IS THAT DOGGIE
IN THE WINDOW?

AZELTON SUB-16 was a door in the sub-basement of the library. None of Artie's AVT keys gave entry to the steam tunnel system that went beneath the buildings of Alabaster; Frankie had tried them on every door she knew. But the key from the back of the *Disreputable History* fit perfectly, and Frankie stepped into the tunnels, alone at lunchtime, the Monday after Alpha's return.

An entry in the *History* from 1963 explained that the steam tunnels of Alabaster crisscrossed the campus, filled with dead ends, occasional manholes, locked doors and hot steam pipes lining the walls. Only janitors and fix-it people were allowed access. A Basset called Shelby Dexter had filched this key from a library maintenance man he'd found asleep on the job, and it had been handed down to every Basset king thereafter.

In 1965, several Bassets claimed to have brought girls from a nearby school down to the tunnels during a holiday dance, to consummate passions unfit for public spaces. In 1967, an enterprising king, possessed of a large amount of money and minimal knowledge of wine, created a significant wine cellar in the tunnels— only to find that within a short period of time, all the bottles had overheated and their contents had spoiled. In 1968, the members of the Loyal Order had launched a systematic infiltration of whatever buildings they could reach through the tunnels, drawing the Basset Hound logo on chalkboards all across campus every night for a week. In the early '70s, during the time the Bassets had most indulged in smoking marijuana, the tunnels had been dank with the sweet and acrid smell of old pot smoke, and in '75, when Frankie's dad was a Basset, the order members had several times infiltrated the building site of the new sciences building, each time leaving behind several stuffed basset hounds in prominent locations.

The autumn air was chill and the Alabaster heating system was already running when Frankie first explored the tunnels. She brought a flashlight with her to avoid flipping any light switches, but within minutes she was sweating so badly she had to leave. She returned later that night with a tank top and shorts under her clothes. In her pocket she had a compass and a ball of twine.

She looped and knotted the twine on a spigot attached to a pipe near the door, switched on her flashlight, and walked quickly into the tunnels, ignoring the pricking feeling down her spine and reminding herself that she wasn't being watched.

It was only the panopticon that was making her feel so paranoid, she said to herself. That, and the guilt of systematically lying to her boyfriend since the day she had first followed him.

The tunnel led Frankie underneath Hazelton—then, as she estimated it, beneath the quad. There were several crossroads, and many of the turns she took led to dead ends. There were relatively few straight lines, as well—the paths twisted and turned at right angles. Frankie relied on the unspooling twine to keep her from getting irremediably lost.

Many of the doors and trapdoors had labels on them, written in black permanent marker in an unofficial scrawl, probably by a series of maintenance men over the years. Frankie found the science buildings, the arts complex, the caf, and so on—but all of them were tightly locked.

It took nearly two hours for her to find a door that opened. When she finally came across it, however, she knew she'd scored: it led to the subbasement of the old gymnasium. She could smell the chlorine soaked into the walls, even though the pool there had been out of use for a decade.

Tying the twine tightly to the door handle and keeping her flashlight low, Frankie mounted the stairs from the subbasement beyond the pool on the basement level, and up to the main floor. There were two large rooms, both with gym floors and basketball courts. Ceilings were double height and windows exceptionally high.

Frankie located the custodian's closet.

She went upstairs.

The top floor had boys' and girls' locker rooms and a weight room. The hallway was lined with windows that looked out onto one of the boys' dormitories.

Frankie looked for outlets. She flicked a light to be sure the electricity was still running.

It was one thirty a.m.

By two fifteen she had followed the twine back into Hazelton, exited through a propped-open basement window, called Trish on her cell, and been admitted through the second-floor kitchen door of her dormitory.

"I hope you're using birth control," whispered Trish grouchily as she crawled back into bed.

Frankie nodded.

"You look awful right now." Trish added. "Are you okay?"

"Sure."

"For real? What are you not telling me?"

There was so much Frankie wasn't telling her. How could she begin?

"Matthew and I had an argument," she lied. "We made up, but it was a whole thing. Actually, I'm going to write about it and sort out my thoughts." She unplugged her laptop and brought it into bed with her. "The light from this won't bother you, will it?"

"No. I'm half asleep already," Trish mumbled. "I'm sorry you had a fight."

"S'okay."

Frankie woke the computer up and checked her wireless connection. Every bone in her body was sore, but she was wide awake. She still had thirteen e-mails to write.

Four days later, beginning at five p.m., the windows of the old gymnasium—both those high ones in the ground-floor basketball courts and the upstairs ones near the locker rooms—were illuminated with twelve two-foot-high plastic basset hounds wearing Santa hats, originally designed as holiday lawn ornaments. They glowed from within.

They came from SantasAnimals.com, and each

one had been ordered by and delivered to a member of the Loyal Order. Extension cords had been purchased by the boys from an online supplier, as had flashlights. The Hazelton subbasement key had been duplicated and found by Alpha Tesorieri in his mailbox, whereupon he did exactly as Frankie told him and led his compatriots down to the basement at four thirty a.m. on the morning of the project. The Bassets followed the twine Frankie had left for them through steamy dark tunnels to the old gymnasium, where they jacked open the custodian's closet with pliers, opened the double-height ladder therein, and supervised the placement of the basset hound holiday lights in all the windows.

Porter was assigned to feign sickness, skip lacrosse practice, and reenter the gym through the steam tunnels shortly before dusk. Once there, he plugged it all in.

When the Alabaster students began walking across campus after sports practice, trickling toward the caf for dinner, a group of people assembled in front of the old gym. They stared at the goofy-looking hounds, which were glowing in the fading light.

Frankie was walking over to pick up Matthew from soccer practice when she saw the crowd. She'd been expecting the dogs, of course, but it hadn't occurred to her that people would congregate in front of the building. She stood, hugging her sweater around her.

"Shocker, huh? How did they get in there?" Star was talking to Claudia.

"I don't know; it's been chained shut since years ago when some seniors snuck in there. My brother told me."

"Aren't they supposed to renovate it?"

"My brother said it's got asbestos," sniffed Claudia.

"I think it's like those dogs are watching us," said Star. "Doesn't it feel creepy?"

Claudia shrugged. "I think whoever's doing it just thinks the campus needs more decoration. Like the pictures needed frilly bras, and the old gym needs Christmas lights."

"Maybe."

"Wasn't there a basset hound on that invite we got to the golf course party, same as on the Halloween letter?"

"I hear it's some kind of secret society doing everything," Star said. "That's what Ash told me."

"Really?"

"Yeah, like it goes way back and nobody knows who's a member."

"But didn't Dean have something to do with that party?"

Star said sulkily, "I don't want to talk about Dean."

"But didn't he?"

"I don't know. He never told me anything about anything."

Claudia shook her head. "I don't think he's smart enough to do something like this."

"What do you mean?" Star snapped. "He's applying early-decision to Princeton."

"Yeah, but he would never think of this," mused Claudia. "Would he? He'd never be motivated enough."

"I told you I don't want to talk about him."

Frankie didn't speak to Star—or to anyone else. She stood there, exhilarated, listening to fifty-four students and three faculty members argue, speculate, and wonder.

About something she had done.

Something she had made happen.

An Ignominious Fall

◉

I N THE MONTH of November, the Loyal
Order of the Basset Hounds experienced a
surge in activity that surpassed anything
they'd accomplished since 1968. All activities were
masterminded by thealphadog@gmail.com. All ideas
were attributed to Alpha, who maintained a mysterious silence as to his methods and spent increasing
amounts of time with Elizabeth, almost to the point
of avoiding his fellow Bassets—and avoiding Matthew
in particular.

Many of what Headmaster Richmond would
later term "mal-doings" were ideas lifted from *The
Disreputable History*. Frankie searched "how to draw"
and "basset hounds" on the Web and came up with an
online tutorial on sketching the dog. She made all the

members of the Order learn to draw a basset, after which they used copies of Artie's keys to enter locked buildings at night and draw large-scale hounds on all the chalkboards.

She had those with unlimited credit cards purchase large quantities of stuffed bassets, which were then displayed, nose to tail, parading from the main building to a prominently located fire hydrant. (She had measured the distance carefully to ensure there were enough stuffed animals to reach all the way.)

On a larger scale, there was the Night of a Thousand Dogs, in which every member of the senior class was mailed a large rubber dog mask. There were no bassets in the bunch—it turned out that there wasn't much market for masks of smaller canines. Instead there were rottweilers, bulldogs, Great Danes, and German shepherds. They were ordered from thirty different Internet sites by the boys. Instructions were subsequently mailed out, and the senior class wore their dog masks to the Harvest Concert one Friday evening (excepting only a few uptight members of student government and the members of the choir).

When the moment came for the all-school sing— "'Tis a Gift to be Simple," followed by "This Land is Your Land"—the dogs tipped their noses to the ceiling and howled. One of them hoisted a sign that read:

```
We respectfully inform you that,
In our collective opinion,
Folk music sucks.
```

The concert ended prematurely.

From: Alessandro Tesorieri [at114@alabasterpreparatory.edu]
To: thealphadog@gmail.com

Hey there, psychopath,
Some of the dogs are asking me why I'm hassling the administration. A line of stuffed animals is one thing, but when you start
messing with the choir teachers, you're going to end up with
enemies.

I don't want to take the flack for this.

> **From:** thealphadog@gmail.com
> **To:** Alessandro Tesorieri [at114@alabasterpreparatory.edu]
>
> Relax. 96% of the senior class participated. The whole
> school is energized.
> Besides, I know you agree with me about folk music.

From: Alessandro Tesorieri [at114@alabasterpreparatory.edu]
To: thealphadog@gmail.com

I want you to stop—now.

> **From:** thealphadog@gmail.com
> **To:** Alessandro Tesorieri [at114@alabasterpreparatory.edu]
>
> No.

From: Alessandro Tesorieri [at114@alabasterpreparatory.edu]
To: thealphadog@gmail.com

I can't get in trouble over this. I can't afford to get in real trouble over this.

> **From:** thealphadog@gmail.com
> **To:** Alessandro Tesorieri [at114@alabasterpreparatory.edu]
>
> You won't get in trouble unless you do something dumb.
> All trails are well covered.

From: Alessandro Tesorieri [at114@alabasterpreparatory.edu]
To: thealphadog@gmail.com

I'm not jumping when you say jump anymore.

> **From:** thealphadog@gmail.com
> **To:** Alessandro Tesorieri [at114@alabasterpreparatory.edu]
>
> Are you going to tell the dogs you're not the guy they think you are?
> Tell Richmond everything and implicate all the dogs who have done your bidding?
> Show Elizabeth you're not the man she thinks she loves?

From: Alessandro Tesorieri [at114@alabasterpreparatory.edu]
To: thealphadog@gmail.com

Fine. You got me. Obviously not.
But I still want that book back, you power-hungry weenie.

> **From:** thealphadog@gmail.com
> **To:** Alessandro Tesorieri [at114@alabasterpreparatory.edu]
>
> You'll like the next mission, Alessandro. I promise you that.

From: Alessandro Tesorieri [at114@alabasterpreparatory.edu]
To: thealphadog@gmail.com

Why are you doing this? That's what I can't figure out.

(No reply.)

From: Alessandro Tesorieri [at114@alabasterpreparatory.edu]
To: thealphadog@gmail.com

You want me to think about you all the time, is that it?

(No reply.)

From: Alessandro Tesorieri [at114@alabasterpreparatory.edu]
To: thealphadog@gmail.com

But what good does it do to have me thinking about you if I don't know who you are?

(No reply.)

From: Alessandro Tesorieri [at114@alabasterpreparatory.edu]
To: thealphadog@gmail.com

Write me back! We're having a conversation here!

(No reply.)

THE CANNED BEET REBELLION

HE CANNED BEET REBELLION originated
when Headmaster Richmond announced at
Chapel that Sylvia Kargman, a particularly
generous alum, CEO of Viva (a large soft drink corporation) and mother to three boys, the middle of whom
(Jeff) was currently an Alabaster junior, was coming to
speak schoolwide on the subject of "Following Your
Dreams: Essential Knowledge and Strategies for
Success." In his preparatory speech, Richmond noted
that Ms. Kargman's company had "sponsored" renova-
tions of the caf.

"You know that's why all the drink machines are
Viva," muttered Matthew as they walked out of
Chapel.

"Are they?" Frankie hadn't noticed.

"Sure. Two years ago they hauled out all the Coke and Snapple machines and replaced them."

"What about the juice machine in the gym?"

"Read the fine print. Jumbo Juice is a product of the Viva Corporation. This whole campus is striped with ads for Jeff's mom's company." (Jeff Kargman was neither a Basset nor a particular friend of any Bassets. He was, in fact, a member of the Geek Club Conglomerate, being active in both the Science Olympiad and the Horticulture Club.)

"What else do they own?" asked Frankie.

Matthew shrugged. "The paper did an article when the caf renovation happened. Viva owns not only Jumbo Juice, but Swell cheese products, NiceFood canned goods, and a company that makes preshaped frozen hamburgers. All things we use in the caf every day. We tried to get people riled up, but nothing happened. The building is air-conditioned now and has pretty skylights, but the caf food still sucks and the school is contracted to use all these processed foods for I don't remember how long."

"You wrote all that stuff and nobody cared?"

"I didn't write it. One of the senior staff did. I was only a sophomore."

"People didn't complain or rebel?"

Matthew put his arm around her. "I've been an editor there almost two years now, and I'm seriously over fooling myself that anybody reads the paper."

"I read it."

"But did you read it before you met me?"

"No."

"No one reads it. It's the irony of my life that editing this thing will get me into college, but nobody actually cares about it at all."

"Is that why there's no salad?"

"In the caf? There's salad."

"Not really. There's garbanzos and canned beets. And pimento olives. Zada says at Berkeley they have this huge salad bar with like, arugula and tomatoes and avocados and snow peas. And maybe ten different dressings."

But Frankie could tell Matthew wasn't listening to her. His eyes were on Steve, who was jogging across the quad toward them. "Dog!" Steve hollered.

"What?"

"Come here, I gotta talk to you about soccer. Sorry, Frankie."

"All right. Baby, I gotta motor." Matthew kissed Frankie on the lips and walked off.

Frankie opened her laptop as soon as she got to class and spent second period inventing the Society for Vegetable Awareness, Promotion, and Information Delegation. Within twenty-four hours, the members of the Loyal

Order, following her directions, had ordered bumper stickers, buttons, and flyers for the afternoon of Sylvia Kargman's lecture. The day of the visit was unofficially declared Vegetable Awareness Day. Every student mailbox received a button; bumper stickers were in every bathroom, and a note was clipped to every clipboard on every dorm room door. The buttons:

WHITHER ART THOU, CAULIFLOWER?

KETCHUP IS NOT A VEGETABLE.

I AM VEGETABLY AWARE.

"Welcome to the Canned Beet Rebellion," read the clipboard note.

```
Today you will unwittingly and possibly
unwantingly participate in
The Canned Beet Rebellion,
under the auspices of
the Society for Vegetable Awareness,
Promotion, and Information Delegation,
in which,
to be quick about it,
we demand a salad bar at both lunch and
dinner in the caf.
Alabaster's current vegetable offerings
are canned and/or anemic. In fact, they
are limp and grodie and not a proper
salad bar.
Viva not the Viva but the Veg!
```

The requested salad bar will include
(on a regular basis):
lettuce and spinach,
cauliflower or broccoli,
carrots or celery,
tomatoes,
cucumbers,
a vegetable of the day,
maybe some fruit,
at least five kinds of salad dressing,
and
those fun bacon-bitty things, which
may or may not be real bacon. We are
prepared to be flexible on this
nonvegetable element of the salad bar.

The Viva Soft Drink Company's products
monopolize the school's food budget
because Viva paid for the renovation of
the caf.
The caf is very nice, but
it needs some salad.
So:
Even if you don't give a $#%* about
salad, wear your VAPID buttons to the
Viva lecture this afternoon. If only to
amuse us, as we have been amusing you.

    (no signature, only the basset hound rubber-stamp,
this time in jolly green ink)

The compliance level astonished even Frankie. Nearly every member of the Alabaster student body wore a button or displayed a bumper sticker plastered across a notebook. The Viva executive's lecture was respectfully received, but at the end an envelope addressed to Ms. Kargman was passed through the chapel, hand over hand. No one knew from whom it originated. Kargman accepted the envelope graciously, opened it, and found a button: "Vegetable of the Day!"

Puzzled, she thanked the student body and wore the button proudly all afternoon.

Shortly before lunch, a Boston caterer arrived on campus to deliver an enormous platter to the central hallway of the main building. When unveiled, the item proved to be a three-foot-by-four-foot image of a basset hound, composed entirely of vegetables. Its droopy eyes were formed by grilled eggplants, its spots by overlapping roasted carrots and red peppers. Crispy jicama was used for the white fur, and the whole thing rested on a charming green background of cucumber, parsley, and broccoli. Underneath the hound was a small note: EAT ME.

Headmaster Richmond, whose office was on the adjoining hall, was seen consuming several pieces of the basset's left foot, in a display of tense good humor.

The following day Ms. Kargman, realizing in retrospect that she had been mocked and criticized, decided upon damage control rather than complaint. She promptly mailed a check to Richmond with a short note saying that student nutrition was important to the Viva corporation—and to her, personally—and she was pleased to make a donation to fund the building of a larger salad bar in the caf, and committed to stocking it with fresh vegetables for the remainder of the school year.

Richmond gave a tedious speech at the next week's Chapel meeting, explaining that there were appropriate and inappropriate ways to express a desire for change in one's community, and there were appropriate and inappropriate ways to express artistic inclinations; and the two were different kinds of expression with different appropriate contexts. However, neither one should involve the infiltration of abandoned buildings, playing with electricity, the mockery of invited guest lecturers, or the delivery of perishable foods to public spaces at inopportune times.

Frankie felt an incredible sense of happiness as Richmond droned on. She was busy—absorbed for the first time, seriously, in what she was doing. Deep in research for her Cities class on the activities of the Suicide Club and the Cacophony Society, scouring the Internet for places to make the Bassets order note cards, bumper stickers, holiday decorations, extension cords, dogs made of vegetables, and the like, she felt a rush of excitement on a daily basis that made her old interests—ultimate Frisbee, modern dance, reading, and debate—seem catatonically dull by comparison. Now she was the commander in chief of a squad of older boys, sending them on adventures that shook Alabaster to its foundations.

That evening, Matthew blew her off for a Basset Hound meeting and Frankie didn't even follow him—because she didn't care.

He might think he had a secret from her, but he didn't.

He was doing exactly what she told him to do.

From: Alessandro Tesorieri [at114@alabasterpreparatory.edu]
To: thealphadog@gmail.com

You were right.
I did like that one.
But you're still a psychopath.
What do you want?

> **From:** thealphadog@gmail.com
> **To:** Alessandro Tesorieri [at114@alabasterpreparatory.edu]
>
> I am getting *exactly* what I want.
> Happy Thanksgiving.

The Return of Bunny Rabbit

◎

MATTHEW HAD GONE quiet about Thanksgiving break. When they'd discussed it in early November, he'd told Frankie he was going home to Boston to celebrate with his parents. She had invited him to come down and visit her on the Friday after the holiday. "Rescue me from Ruth," Frankie told him, hoping the idea of being her savior would override his lack of interest in meeting her family. "Because I may come back mentally deranged if I'm left alone with her for four days. Zada is staying in California."

Matthew had said yes. Of course he'd rescue her. He'd drive down and take her out to see a show in New York City.

But he hadn't mentioned it since.

And he kept not mentioning it as the holiday grew close.

"Are you coming to rescue me?" she finally asked him two days before the break. They were sitting in the library after dinner. Matthew had bought Frankie three rolls of strawberry Mentos, and they had opened them up and arranged the candies in a row between them while they studied. "Because my mother is going to be driving me crazy."

"If I can get away, I definitely will," Matthew said. "Alpha wants to go do this crazy Alpine slide thing in western Mass."

"What is it?"

"He's a madman. You slide down these mountains on carts, like a baby bobsled with no snow."

A cold spot formed in Frankie's chest. "Can I come?" she asked.

"Oh, um." Matthew ran a hand through his hair. "That would be great. But how will we get you?"

"Can you pick me up?"

"Not on Thursday night; my family's dinner never even starts till nine."

"I could take the bus to Boston Friday morning."

"Um. I think we're leaving early."

"Can't you go later?"

"You have to get there early, Alpha says."

"Matthew."

277

"What?"

"You already made this plan, then."

"Kind of."

"But didn't we talk about you coming to New Jersey on Friday?"

"Yeah."

"So I thought you were driving down, probably."

"I was, I—this came up, and I promised Alpha. You and I didn't fix anything certain, did we?"

"No. It's—I'll miss you." She felt like she never got him alone. Felt like she was always in his world and he was never in hers. And here was evidence: that no matter how hard she pushed herself into his world—heck, she was running whole sections of his life at this point, not that he knew—no matter how hard she pushed her way in, he could always close a door on her.

"I'll miss you too," Matthew said, taking a strawberry Mento and feeding it to her. "But we'll see each other Sunday night. Call me as soon as you're on campus."

Frankie ate the candy. The touch of his fingers on her lips distracted her. He had brought her strawberry Mentos, after all.

Shouldn't that be enough?

Matthew stood up to go to the bathroom down the hall, and while he was gone, Frankie looked in his backpack. It was wrong, she knew. But she felt like she was losing her grip on him. Two notebooks—calculus and history of Japan. Several pens, including highlighters. Three chocolate wrappers, and a roll of quarters. A letter from his mother, still unopened. A cough drop. A number of old flyers: a school calendar for October, a list of open electives, a memo about plagiarism. And a printout.

In Matthew's backpack was a printout of the e-mails between Frankie and Porter, just going this far:

From: Porter Welsch [pw034@alabasterpreparatory.edu]
To: Frances Landau-Banks [fl202@alabasterpreparatory.edu]
Subject: Hey

Frankie, what's up? Hope your term is going well so far. I want to apologize for what happened with Bess last year.
—Porter

> **From:** Frances Landau-Banks
>   [fl202@alabasterpreparatory.edu]
> **To:** Porter Welsch [pw034@alabasterpreparatory.edu]
> **Subject:** Re: Hey
>
> You mean, you *want* to apologize, or you *are* apologizing? Your grammar is indistinct.

That was it.

Frankie shoved the printout back into the bag and returned to studying. Matthew returned and fed her another Mento.

She couldn't ask him about it.

If she did, he'd know she'd looked in his backpack.

Frankie sunk into her chair, a tangle of guilt and anger—but she didn't say a word.

Frankie spent Thanksgiving break in New Jersey with Ruth, her uncles, and the vile male cousins. Zada called from California, and Senior from Boston, to wish them all a happy holiday.

"How's our Bunny Rabbit liking school?" asked Uncle Ben, ruffling Frankie's hair as she offered him a cup of hot apple cider. Ruth was in the kitchen making gravy.

"It's good."

"Great."

Uncle Paul came over and squeezed Frankie's shoulders. "You got so tall since the summer. Did you start high school at that fancy place your dad's so proud of?"

"I'm a sophomore, Uncle Paul."

Uncle Paul pretended disbelief. "You're kidding me. There's no way you're a sophomore. Last year, I swear it on my grave, I was changing your diapers."

"I agree," said Ben. "Just yesterday, I tell you, she was dragging that dolly everywhere, you remember, the one with no arms?"

Ruth came out of the kitchen and wrapped her

arms around Frankie. "She's as adorable as always, though, don't you think?"

"You got a boyfriend there at your fancy school?" Uncle Paul wanted to know. "Your mother says you have a boyfriend."

"Mom!"

Ruth looked innocent. "I wasn't supposed to tell?"

Paulie Junior had found a tray of desserts hidden in the den and was stuffing chocolate jellies into his mouth, but he stopped long enough to chant: "Frankie's got a boyfriend, Frankie's got a boyfriend."

Frankie smirked at Ruth. "You don't have to broadcast it."

"It's a secret from your own family you have a boyfriend?" Ruth waved her hands dismissively. "I'm glad you have a nice guy to take care of you up there." Ruth looked at Ben. "Zada says he's from a very good family. Newspaper people."

"Yeah, it's a good family," muttered Frankie.

"He's nicer than that one you had last year, right, Bunny?" asked Uncle Paul. "I seem to remember there was some hocus-pocus with that one."

"You mean hanky-panky!" shouted Ruth. "There was hanky-panky."

"There was *not*," moaned Frankie.

"Anyway, this one's better, right, Bunny?" said Ruth. "He treats her well, Zada told me. Takes care of you?"

"He's not a babysitter, Mom."

"A babysitter? Who's talking about babysitters?"

"You act like I need a boyfriend to take care of me."

"That's not what I'm saying," said Ruth, busying herself mixing butter into a bowl of mashed potatoes. "I'm a feminist like anyone. I'm just saying—"

"What?"

"I didn't worry about you at school when Zada was there. But now you're there all alone, I like thinking you have this nice guy to watch out for you— that's all."

"You always underestimate me."

Ruth shook her head. "I think the world of you. Now, can you carry the potatoes out to the table? The bowl is very heavy."

THE FISH LIBERATION SOCIETY

AWAY FROM HER boyfriend for four days and feeling neglected, Frankie reasoned through the meaning of what she'd found in his backpack thus: if Matthew had looked at the Frankie–Porter e-mails on Frankie's laptop, he wouldn't have been able to print them out—unless he'd forwarded them to himself for later use. Frankie checked her sent-mail folder, and he hadn't. Unless he'd thought to erase the sent-mail record.

More likely, she figured, Matthew had seen the e-mails on *Porter's* laptop—but even then, he would also have had to forward them, and in any case, where they were forwarded for printing, the e-mails would read as forwards, whereas these printed out clean, no trace of Matthew's e-mail address.

So. Porter had given him a printout.

Yes, that was the most likely conclusion. Porter had given Matthew a copy of those e-mails. But why?

Could Matthew have forced Porter to apologize to Frankie? And demanded that Porter deliver him a copy of the apology? However, Porter must have then committed the insubordination of asking Frankie to lunch in order to warn her against Matthew.

That would explain why Matthew had been so upset about Frankie going to lunch with Porter. According to the hierarchy of the Bassets, Matthew was supposed to control Porter—but Porter had proven himself unwilling to be completely controlled.

If Frankie had done what Matthew asked of her and stood Porter up, that would have been a win for Matthew. But as it was, she had gone to lunch against his wishes—and Porter had gained some power. Though Frankie never told Matthew that Porter had warned her against him, Porter's defiant lunch invitation marked him as the least loyal of the Basset Hounds. As such, he was a potential liability.

Something to remember.

Though she was pleased with the conclusions she drew from her reasoning, Frankie wandered around her mother's house in the days after Thanksgiving, staring out of windows for long periods of time. The knowledge that Matthew had forced Porter to make the apology hung over her like a damp wash-cloth.

She ate too many brownies and felt a little sick to her stomach. She opened books and didn't read past the first page.

She wished Matthew would call. But he didn't.

The Loyal Order's next large-scale venture occurred in early December. It was the kidnapping of the Alabaster Guppy and its replacement with a large plastic lawn ornament in the shape of a sad-eyed basset hound. The basset came with a plastic sign at its feet that had previously contained the phrase, "Consciousness: That Annoying Time Between Naps!" It now featured a notice, carefully laminated in case of rain:

```
Sprung free of its bonds by members
of the Fish Liberation Society, the
Alabaster Guppy will journey to its
natural home at the bottom of the pond,
unless it can be convinced to return
upon delivery of a ransom. More to
follow.
```

A ransom note was then delivered to Headmaster Richmond, printed in block letters on an adorable card of a basset hound wearing a stethoscope, the inside of which had formerly read, "All those doctors can go to the dogs! Get well soon."

The note demanded the cessation of mandatory Chapel on Monday mornings:

The Guppy feels that the implied Christianity of required Chapel attendance, even though the assemblies are technically nondenominational, is an affront to those Alabaster students who are Jewish, Buddhist, Muslim, or whatever else. Mandatory Chapel is also highly irksome to those who, like the Guppy himself, prefer to consider themselves atheists.

The Guppy defends each student's right to hear about sports schedules, charity initiatives, and school dances without the big pictures of Jesus on the cross dominating the proceedings. Even for Christian students, it is inappropriate to mix religious awe with announcements concerning the PSATs.

The Guppy respectfully requests that school assemblies be henceforth held in the auditorium of the new arts complex. It will be pleased to return when this change has been made.

Photocopies of this note were delivered to every mailbox.

Richmond responded by calling a meeting of the faculty, during which considerable discussion ensued. The question of assembly in the chapel had been brought up before, but Alabaster tradition had prevailed against the small number of non-Christian or atheist students who had asked for a switch, and those had been easily cowed by Richmond's assertion that the stained glass crucifixions and Virgins were part of the Alabaster tradition students had enjoyed for nearly 120 years, and that since the content of the assembly was explicitly nonreligious, no one could possibly object.

The students had proposed noncompulsory attendance, and indeed that had been tried in 1998, but numbers at assembly had subsequently dropped so low that no one knew when events were scheduled, membership in school activities and charity drives diminished, and a quantity of students got into all kinds of trouble on Monday morning while most of the faculty members were attending morning assembly.

So mandatory Chapel had been reinstated, and no one had seriously questioned it in the twenty-first century.

The Guppy statue had been at Alabaster since its third year and was an object of wealthy alumni nostalgia. During its 1951 sojourn at the home of seminal

Basset Hound Hardewick's mother, the Old-Boy outrage at its loss was both vitriolic and impassioned.

Now, Headmaster Richmond convened a faculty meeting to discuss the contents of Frankie's note. Some members argued that the bad behavior of stealing the Guppy should not be encouraged. The perpetrators should be located and suspended. Others argued that if the requests of the organization now calling itself the Fish Liberation Society were ignored, the Guppy might never be retrieved. Alumni disappointment would be considerable—and that could cause financial damage to the school, which was heavily dependent on contributions. Also, what if the perpetrator were the son or daughter of a major alum? It was safer and quieter to capitulate.

Still, other faculty members argued that assembly in the chapel had always bothered them as well, either because the chapel should be reserved for religious worship or because the chapel's atmosphere of devout Christianity was oppressive to those with other religious affiliations, as these fish people—vegetable people, dog people, breast people, whatever they were—had pointed out.

In the end, Richmond posted a notice moving Monday morning assembly to the new arts complex auditorium, effective immediately, and demanding the return of the Guppy.

That afternoon, around five o'clock, Elizabeth Heywood received a typewritten note under her door, directing her and several of her girlfriends on a scavenger hunt for the Guppy. The first clue led them to Richmond's office, where a second clue led them to the offices of the physical plant; and before long, a trail of administrators, janitors, gym teachers, and underclassmen were following the senior girls as they figured out a series of paper puzzles. Movie night went unattended, study groups disbanded, and the headmaster canceled a date with his wife.

Frankie, Matthew, and Alpha followed Elizabeth until she reached the final clue:

```
Under water I am not
But you're finally getting hot
My tub with chlorine
Once was deep
Now it's dry
And there I sleep.
```

The Guppy was in the empty swimming pool of the old gymnasium.

A janitor opened the chained door after a fifteen-minute wait, and half the school swarmed into the abandoned building. Frankie reached out and squeezed Matthew's hand. "The swimming pool. Perfect," she said.

He chuckled. "It's not bad."

"What do you think it means?" Frankie asked.

She really wanted to know. It had been more than a month now, her plotting these escapades and the members of the Loyal Order executing them. And though she took a deep satisfaction in her work and the reaction people had to it, she had begun to hunger for a chance to discuss the projects. She'd expended terrific effort to make these things happen, and she wanted to talk about them with Matthew, whose opinion she valued most.

"Hm?" He seemed distracted.

"Putting the Guppy in the old pool. Don't you think it means something?"

"How so?"

She couldn't believe he'd hauled this several-hundred-pound statue through sweltering underground tunnels in the middle of the night without ever considering the symbolism of the hiding place. "The Guppy is this icon of our school, right? All the alumni remember it fondly, it's been here forever, etcetera."

"Yeah."

"So?"

"What?"

"Don't you see?"

"Well, it's a guppy in a pool, and that's kind of like a fish tank," Matthew said.

"Isn't it a symbol of the old Alabaster being obsolete?"

"Maybe." Matthew laughed and put his arm around Frankie. "But maybe you're thinking too much."

"No, seriously," she persisted. "The Guppy represents the old-fashioned values of the school, and putting it in the dry pool is like saying those values are old and useless, the way the pool is."

"What values?"

Why was he not understanding her? Was he playing dumb to keep the secret? "The whole Alabaster network, prep school Old Boy thing," she told him.

"Seems to me like you're reading a lot into nothing." Matthew shrugged.

"Don't you think that's what's getting shook up here?"

"You mean, shaken up?"

He was correcting her grammar.

She was explaining this whole prank to him, the prank he'd actually carried out, and instead of listening to her point, he was correcting her grammar. "You're thinking too much," he had said.

What? He didn't want her to think?

What was the point of doing *any* of these pranks if people weren't going to think about them?

"Yeah," Frankie said. "Shaken up."

Matthew stroked her hair. "You're adorable. You know I think that, right?"

"Thanks," said Frankie.

The sad thing was, she did know. But it wasn't enough.

He leaned in and kissed her neck. "You smell good, too. You want to come shake me up for a few minutes before curfew? Let's be alone."

He was bringing up the grammar thing again.

He just wanted to make out—he wasn't ever going to listen to what she wanted to say. He didn't know they were in this together.

Matthew thought he and the Basset Hounds had made this happen on their own—and he wasn't going to tell her about it no matter how interested Frankie showed him she was.

It wasn't that he no longer had a secret from her. In fact, Matthew's secret was getting bigger and bigger—and Frankie finally had to admit to herself that he wasn't ever, ever going to tell her.

She turned to him. "I can't believe you just said that, Matthew. Shake you up?"

"Aw, I didn't mean it that way. We were joking around—shook up, shaken up?"

"Right."

"Don't be mad."

"Fine."

"Come on."

"I'm not mad," she lied. "I just remembered there's something I gotta do."

TWINE

◉

FRANKIE HEADED for the library. She had left the twine running from the door of Hazelton sub-16 through the maze of overheated tunnels to the old gymnasium. She had done the same thing after the Doggies in the Window project, and at that time had scolded herself for forgetting to have someone roll it up. If the janitorial staff found the twine, it would be a matter of hours before the lock on sub-16 was changed, so it was crucial that the twine be wound up—but not a single Basset had thought to do it without being told. Frankie had skipped a class to take care of it when she was sure no members of the Loyal Order would be around to catch her.

Perversely, the dogs' incompetence had made her happy.

They needed her, she thought as she navigated the steam tunnels with a flashlight under one arm. She was their mastermind.

She had also liked the small opportunity for physical participation afforded her by the steam tunnel escapades. She liked laying out the twine and rolling it up. So many of her efforts in the adventures of the Loyal Order were conducted on her laptop and in the printer lab, while the boys scaled buildings, ran extension cords, or went shopping.

So in planning the relocation of the Guppy to the swimming pool via the tunnels, Frankie had always intended to roll up the twine herself.

As she slipped into the Hazelton basement, after leaving Matthew at the scene in the old gymnasium, she kept her flashlight off. She dropped her wool coat, sweater, and thermal near the entrance, stripping down to a tank top and jeans. She ran her hand along the taut twine. When she got to the old gymnasium, she would untie that end and reroll it as she returned to the library.

The tunnels were noisy with the hiss and banging of steam heat in pipes. It was hotter at night—when the heat had been running for some sixteen hours—than it was during the day. Frankie began to sweat, and found as she threaded her way through the dark that instead of feeling superior and involved, as she had last time she'd rolled up the twine—she felt lonely.

No one cared enough about the projects of the Loyal Order to think of doing this chore. Matthew didn't care enough to think through the symbolism of the latest prank. What they cared about, really, she thought to herself, was their secrecy. Their clubbiness.

She could command them, outwit them; she could know more of their history than any of them ever would—but they would preserve that secrecy and clubbiness against her even so.

The projects didn't matter to Matthew, Frankie thought. Sure he liked them, he admired them, he thought they were fun and clever, but what mattered to him was executing them with his buddies. What mattered was that thrill of rebellion and unconventionality without risking the solid security of privilege.

He likes it better when it's just a guppy in a pool, or a doggie in a window, she thought. Not anything more. Not anything symbolic. He doesn't want to change the way things work; doesn't seriously want to anger the administration or question authority. He wants to drink beer on the golf course with his friends. And so do the rest of them.

That's why he wouldn't analyze the pranks with me, when he's a guy who likes to analyze everything, she thought. He doesn't want them to mean anything that would destabilize his world. Even the thing about the Viva corporation—he was annoyed about it, but he

wasn't interested in changing the status quo by editori-
alizing in the paper, because that would have shook
things up too much.

Shaken.

Shaken things up.

Frankie had been walking for five minutes when the
twine under her fingers went slack.

What?

How could it be slack? It was quadruple-knotted
to the handle on the door of the old gymnasium. There
was no way it could simply have come untied.

Someone was at the other end.

Rolling up the twine.

Someone *had* cared enough to come down and put
it away.

Someone had cared.

And now he was going to discover her in the tunnels.

Frankie's first impulse was to hide. She let go of
the twine and slammed herself up against a wall, but
her bare arm hit a steam pipe and she could hear the
sizzle even before she felt the pain of the burn. She
leaped away, pressing her own hand over her mouth to
keep herself from crying, switched on her flashlight,
and ran as fast as she could toward the library exit.

Hiding was dumb anyhow. She had to get to the

door and get her coat and clothes so the person behind her in the dark wouldn't find them and know she'd been there.

With ragged breath, she reached the door. As she bent down to grab her jacket and clothes, she saw what she should have seen on her way in—hanging from a nail against the wall was a navy blue peacoat, such as most of the boys at Alabaster wore through the winter. Hastily, and with arms full, Frankie grabbed the door handle, dropping her flashlight and several things out of her pocket in the process. She felt her jacket quickly to make sure her wallet was still there and left what she had dropped. She launched herself into the fluorescent glow of the Hazelton subbasement, bolted up the stairs to the basement-level stacks and buried herself behind a bookshelf, hastily pulling her thermal over her head to hide the seared skin of her arm.

It was quiet.

Had he heard her footsteps? Or the closing of the sub-16 door?

Had he felt her touch on the twine behind him?

There was a jangle of keys, and a pair of security guards trotted through the stacks in the direction of the subbasement entrance. Frankie grabbed a book off a shelf and feigned immersion, looking up only as they passed her. "Hi there," she said.

"Hello." The guard was businesslike.

"Is anything going on down there?"

"Not to worry about. Headmaster thinks whoever stole that statue was transporting it through tunnels that link up with the subbasement, so we're going to check it out," said the guard.

Frankie forced a laugh. "You think someone carried that huge thing into the library with nobody noticing?"

"Probably not. The tunnels down there, they connect most of the buildings on campus. They coulda brought it in any which way. But he told us to go down there and take a look, and this is the nearest entrance from the security desk. Maybe we'll get a hint who's been doing all the vandalism around school lately."

"Vandalism?"

"You know, what with the brassieres on the paintings and those Christmas decorations and such."

"I never thought of it as vandalism."

"We're going down there now, little lady. Duty calls. But don't you worry your pretty head about a thing, you hear?" said the guard, and he and his coworker trotted down the stairs, keys jingling.

BURN

FRANKIE RAN BACK to her dorm and thrust as much of her arm as she could into an ice-cold shower. The skin was beginning to bubble, and a welt ran from above her elbow down to her wrist and across the back of her hand.

It did not escape her notice that this was the second time she'd burned herself on behalf of the Loyal Order.

It was nearly curfew. Her jeans were wet in the spray of the shower, and Frankie was shivering from the cold—but every time she took her arm out of the water the burning sensation was so intense she shoved it back in again.

It hurt.

It hurt.

There were footsteps in the hall, and the bathroom

door began to open. Frankie ducked herself all the way into the stall so no one would see her and wonder why she was standing halfway in the shower. Once under the spray, her jeans felt instantly heavy and water-logged. She wrestled them off and pushed them to the edge of the stall with her foot.

Two girls came into the bathroom—Star and Trish. They were brushing their teeth and rubbing their faces with lotion before bed.

"So I don't understand why they took the Guppy in the first place," Star was saying.

Trish's voice came: "I think the idea is to get everyone talking. Whoever's doing this just wants attention."

"But if they just want attention, why not say who they are?"

"You saw how furious Richmond was, didn't you?"

There was silence for a moment while Trish and Star brushed. Frankie's skin felt raw and frozen. She turned the water to warm, but her burn screamed in protest, so she turned it back to cold, teeth chattering. "I saw he was mad," said Star finally, "but I left when Dean and those guys were helping carry the Guppy back where it belonged. So I missed the speech."

"Oh. You missed this long über-headmaster ramble about theft and insurrection and how disrespectful these Snoopy pranks were to the school administration. Snoopy pranks, that's what he called them."

"So clueless," said Star. "He doesn't even know what's going on in his own school. Anyone can see it's a basset hound."

"Yeah. So then he said he's calling in advisers to school security, to help figure out who the perpetrators are."

"Really?"

"He said Halloween pranks were one thing," Trish went on, "but stealing school property was another, and he was taking the situation extremely seriously."

"So someone's in major trouble."

"Oh, very major. Although I thought it was all clever, actually. Putting this symbol of Alabaster in this crusty old empty pool. Like a commentary," Trish said.

"Uh-huh. What do you think of Elizabeth Heywood's hair?" wondered Star. "Do you think she colored it when she was on TV?"

When Star and Trish left the bathroom, Frankie flipped the water off and stood there shaking, wearing only her wet tank top and underpants.

Her wool jacket hung on the towel hook. She grabbed it and picked up her soaked jeans from the floor of the shower and her shoes from under a bench. Someone had left a large jar of petroleum jelly on a shelf, and she scooped out a handful and wiped it down her burned arm. She pulled some paper towels from the roller and dried the rest of herself as best she could.

Burning and dripping and freezing, Frankie Landau-Banks walked down the hall to her bedroom. Trish was sitting in bed, wearing flannel pajamas decorated with palominos and reading a brochure called "Adventure Kayaking Tours." "What happened to you?" she asked.

"I fell in the pond," lied Frankie.

"How did it happen?"

"My foot slipped."

"You must be freezing. But why did you take your shoes and pants off?" Trish got up to take Frankie's jacket and wet clothes from her. "You didn't walk home like *that*, did you?"

"No, no. I took them off in the bathroom."

"Why didn't you come in here and get a towel?" Trish's eyes widened. "What happened to your arm?"

"Oh, nothing, that's from yesterday."

"You're lying to me."

Frankie peeled off the rest of her clothes. "No, I'm not."

"I'm not dumb, Frankie. You have a huge burn on your arm and your coat's not even wet. There's no mud anywhere. It's obvious you didn't fall in the pond."

Frankie was naked now, rummaging in her

drawer for a sweatshirt and pajama bottoms. "I can't discuss it."

"Why not?" Trish pushed. "Does this have to do with when I got you Artie's keys?"

"No. That was separate."

"What happened to your arm?"

Frankie was in her nightclothes now, and she dove into bed and shut out the lights. "Don't ask me, Trish. Please leave me alone."

"I thought we were friends," Trish pouted.

"We are friends."

"So?"

"So please, my friend. Stay out of it."

"Do you tell Matthew all your secrets now, is that it? And he tells you his?"

"No." Frankie couldn't help but laugh. "Really, you couldn't be more wrong."

"Because I have been with Artie for almost ten months at this point, and I never closed you out like this, Frankie, just because I got a boyfriend. I steal keys for you, lie to Artie for you; I let you in at night when you break your curfew, I lie to the hall monitor for you. I even had breakfast with that pompous Alpha," cried Trish. "And you won't even tell me what's going on."

"You don't like Alpha?" It was inconceivable to Frankie that someone could dislike Alpha, even though part of her hated him deeply.

"Ugh, no," answered Trish. "He thinks he's such a big man on campus."

"How can you not like Alpha?" mused Frankie, feeling slightly delusional and dehydrated.

"How are we going to be real friends, Frankie? That's what I want to know," snapped Trish. "If you lie to me and won't tell me your secrets, huh? How can we be friends that way?"

"I'm a bad friend," moaned Frankie, shivering with chill and pain. "I know it. I'm a horrible friend. I'm sorry. I just—I don't know how to be anything else right now."

Trish sighed. "Do you need some ice?" she asked after a minute. "I'll get you some ice from the machine in the basement."

A Perpetrator

S HORTLY BEFORE CURFEW that night, as the student body would find out the next morning, security guards entered the steam tunnels through a usually locked door in the subbasement of Hazelton library.

Immediately the guards discovered a flashlight, a pack of cinnamon gum, an ultimate Frisbee schedule folded in quarters, a book, a boy's peacoat, and a length of twine near the entrance, the latter with one end tied to a spigot for no explicable reason. A further search revealed senior scholarship student Alessandro Tesorieri, concealing himself in a little-used side passage and sweating profusely.

Tesorieri refused to say what he was doing in the tunnels, but security theorized to Headmaster

Richmond that he was guilty of perpetrating the various activities of the so-called Fish Liberation Society and the alleged Society for Vegetable Awareness, Promotion, and Information Delegation. Tesorieri was also suspected of masterminding other recent infractions—namely the In the Ladies We Trust campaign (including the Library Lady), the Night of a Thousand Dogs, and what had been popularly termed the "Doggies in the Window."

He was charged with theft, vandalism of school property, trespassing, and disrupting the peace. Headmaster Richmond, along with the chief of campus security, questioned Tesorieri, asking him the significance of the dog symbol that appeared on so many of the pranks, linking them together.

Tesorieri merely shrugged and said he'd never much liked Snoopy.

Before they released him, security did a search of Tesorieri's dorm room and laptop. All of these were found to be completely clear of evidence (he had deleted all e-mails, per Frankie's instruction), but at the end of the evening a security guard thought to open the book that had been found near the suspect's peacoat in the tunnels, though the suspect vehemently denied it belonged to him, pointing out also that he neither chewed cinnamon gum nor played ultimate Frisbee.

The book, upon further examination, bore the title

The Disreputable History of the Loyal Order of the Basset Hounds. Its presence next to the suspect's coat was deemed incriminating.

Finally the security officers let Tesorieri go to bed, threatening a formal meeting of the Committee on Student Discipline as soon as it could be arranged.

Frankie went to first and second period the next morning, but she'd barely slept the night before and her arm had begun to swell and ooze, so by third period she was in the nurse practitioner's office making up a lie about an exposed pipe down in the laundry room of the dormitory and receiving a prescription for antibiotics. She felt weak and dizzy.

At lunchtime, Matthew visited her. She was alone, resting on an infirmary bed with three ice packs strapped to her arm with first-aid tape. The nurse was in the front office.

Matthew pulled a chair over to her bed and sat down. "How'd you know I was here?" she asked him.

"Trish told me."

"I asked her not to."

"You ran off last night like you were mad at me."

She could barely remember. Oh, yes. He hadn't listened to her about the Guppy, he'd corrected her grammar, and then he'd suggested she shake him up. He had secrets from her that he wasn't ever revealing.

Matthew had been Frankie's boyfriend for almost three months now. Why couldn't she tell him she was mad? "I don't think we really talk," she mumbled.

"Yes we do," he said, raising his eyes to the ceiling. "We talk all the time."

"I—I think you underestimate me."

"That's not true."

"Yes," Frankie said. "You do. You underestimate me."

Matthew was confused. "I think you're great, Frankie. Charming and funny, and—usually you're adorable. How could I underestimate you?"

"But you do," she told him. "I know you do."

"How can you know?"

"We don't tell each other much, do we?"

He stood and paced the room. "I didn't know we were going to have a relationship talk. I came here to find out if you were okay. And to tell you about Alpha."

"We're not having a relationship talk."

"We're not? Because it sounds like it to me."

"What happened to Alpha?"

"You know how the Guppy got stolen, and there were those basset hound lights in the windows of the old gym?"

"Yeah." Was he going to tell her?

He was. He had to.

He was finally going to tell her.

"And the whole thing with the salad bar and the bras everywhere on Halloween?" Matthew continued.

"Uh-huh."

"It turns out Alpha's been the one making all that happen. He's not telling anyone in the administration anything, but they caught him in the steam tunnels last night and they know that was how the Guppy got to the swimming pool—through the tunnels. They found a notebook in his possession that proved everything."

"In his possession?"

"Well, on the floor next to his other stuff. He says it's not his, but it's pretty much got to be."

So it *was* Alpha in the tunnels.

Some part of Frankie felt pleased. Not that Alpha had been caught—but pleased that she had made him care. That it had been he in the tunnels, winding up twine.

The only better person would have been Matthew.

"What's happening now?" she asked.

"The discipline committee met this morning. They voted to expel him."

"No." Frankie's mind reeled. She hadn't intended this, hadn't meant to ruin him.

"Anyone else, they probably wouldn't expel," Matthew went on. "They'd just threaten, but not really do it. Alpha they can seriously get rid of, so they're going to make him an example. He's expendable in their eyes."

"Why?"

"He's got no money. I mean, his mother doesn't. If it were anyone else, the discipline committee would just make threats. Then the family would make an enormous donation—and the kid would be reinstated with a clean record."

"Not if it were me," said Frankie. "My dad doesn't have that kind of money."

Matthew shrugged. "Well, most people here do. And your dad's an active alum; he knows people. But not Alpha. His mother never even went to college."

"Didn't she take him on a yoga retreat? Isn't that like an expensive spa vacation?"

"She a crazy lady. She's spending through the money she gets from renting out their apartment like there's no tomorrow. She's got no savings, no way of making a living. And Alpha got in early-action to Harvard."

"He did?"

"The letter came last week. But if he gets expelled, he'll lose his place."

"Did you know about all this?" Frankie asked.

"What?"

"Alpha doing all these pranks?" (Tell me, she thought. Tell me.)

Matthew shook his head. "I had no idea."

"But he's your best friend."

"Well, he's completely brilliant—and he always breaks rules and thinks of ideas. I can't say I'm surprised. But the pranks he did this year were way beyond what he did before, and it all kind of had this political slant to it, and an art element, you know? So I didn't know for sure. And it was strange that he didn't tell me."

"Yeah."

"Richmond called me and some of the guys in to see if we knew who was helping Alpha execute the pranks, but there was nothing to say. We didn't know anything."

He was lying to her.

Even now when she was in the infirmary. Even now when she'd told him they didn't really talk.

When Alpha was getting kicked out of school.

"He's not saying a word about how anything went down," continued Matthew. "I thought maybe Elizabeth had been helping him, but now it looks like it was some sophomore he knew."

"Who?"

"Your old boyfriend. Porter Welsch. He got scared and turned in some e-mails he'd got from Alpha, e-mails telling him to buy lawn ornaments and dog masks off the Internet, and to climb the library dome with a parachute."

"Porter worked for Alpha and turned e-mails in to Richmond?"

"I guess so. Anyway, we're all gonna write letters and attest that Alpha's an upstanding citizen and a valuable member of the Alabaster community and all that—but I seriously doubt it'll help. Richmond wants a scapegoat."

Matthew would never tell her, Frankie could see.

And worse, he would never suspect her. Because to him, as to her family, she was Bunny Rabbit. Even though he never called her that.

Harmless.

"Look at my arm, Matthew." Frankie raised herself on her good elbow and lifted the ice pack so he could see the burn.

"Shocker." He came over and took her hand. "What happened to you? I should have asked right away. I'm sorry."

Frankie looked into his face. He genuinely liked her, she knew. Maybe even loved her. He just loved her in a limited way.

Loved her best when she needed help.

Loved her best when he could set the boundaries and make the rules.

Loved her best when she was a smaller, younger person than he was, with no social power. When he could adore her for her youth and charm and protect her from the larger concerns of life. "I burned myself," she said.

"How?"

"You don't have any idea?"

He looked at her arm for a long time. Wrapped in ice packs. "No, I don't. Am I supposed to?"

Frankie took a deep breath and said it. "I burned myself in the steam tunnels."

"What?"

"You're standing here, telling me about Alpha getting caught in the steam tunnels, having spent half of yesterday in the steam tunnels yourself, and you look at my burned arm and it doesn't once cross your mind that I might have been in there with you?"

Matthew dropped her hand. "You followed us?"

"No."

"Then what?"

"Why is it so hard for you to see me, Matthew? Why does it seem so impossible to you that I sent you there? That I wrote the e-mails?"

He stared at her silently.

"It's not hard to get an e-mail address that makes you look like someone else," she told him. "Anyone can do that."

"But why would you?" he whispered.

"I never wanted anyone to get expelled, you have to believe me. I wanted to—" Frankie searched for the right words. "I wanted to—prove myself. I wanted to make things happen, wanted to show that I'm as smart as any of you, or smarter even, when all you ever think is that I'm adorable."

Matthew shook his head.

"I didn't want to be left out," she went on. "You and your club. You're so *exclusionary*, Matthew, it was driving me crazy. That I could be your girlfriend all this time and you'd never tell me, never let me in. Like you thought I wasn't worthy."

"How did you know about the Bassets?" His voice was tight.

"I followed you one night. Into the theater. It wasn't rocket science."

He shivered. "That's crazy."

"What, I should have just asked you to invite me along?"

"Maybe."

"Be real. You wouldn't even let me touch that stupid china doggie in your bedroom. No way were you just going to tell me everything that was going on."

"We told Elizabeth."

"Just enough so she'd make pretty party invitations for you! Not so she'd actually be a part of things."

"Well, we told her. And maybe I would have told you." He was defensive.

"But you didn't, Matthew. I gave you a hundred

chances, and you never did." Frankie swallowed hard. "I wanted to show you what I could do. And there was no way to show you except for this. I thought you'd guess a long time ago, actually. The thing that makes me saddest is that you never did."

She hoped, she hoped, he would *understand*. That he would appreciate her the way he appreciated Alpha. Admire her cleverness, her ambition, her vision. That he would admit her as his equal, or even as his superior, and love her for what she was capable of.

She hoped, she hoped that he would see how badly she wanted to be part of his world, how badly she'd wanted to break through the door that separated them, and how much she deserved to break through it.

"That's seriously sick," Matthew finally said.

It hung in the air.

Matthew unwrapped a piece of gum and stuck it savagely into his mouth, then crumpled the wrapper into a tiny ball. "I can't believe you've been lying to me like this."

"But you were lying to me!" Frankie cried.

"I was not."

"You lied about where you were going, you lied about knowing Porter, you pretended you had nothing to do with anything that happened. You've been lying to me every single day since we met."

"I was being loyal." Matthew stood and walked to

the other end of the infirmary. "Loyal to a group of guys I've known for four years, if not since childhood. Loyal to a society that's existed for more than fifty years. What were you being loyal to, huh? Or were you jerking people around to make yourself feel powerful?"

"I—"

"And what do you have against Alpha? Why would you set him up that way, when he's my best friend? The guy is being expelled because of you."

"I didn't want that to happen! And it's not like he wasn't part of it, too. He never stood up and said he didn't write the e-mails. He could have done that any second. And besides, it's not like you did nothing yourself," cried Frankie. "You stole the Guppy. You rubber-stamped all those letters, and bought bras and toy basset hounds and holiday lights. I know you did. Why aren't you standing up and telling your part in it if you're so concerned about Alpha?"

"I would," shouted Matthew. "But he doesn't freaking want me to. He's the one with the *Disreputable History*, he's the one whose name is on the e-mails, he's the one Porter turned in. Me confessing that I'm a member of the Loyal Order isn't going to change anything except it'll cost my dad a ton of money. There's no point."

Frankie was holding back tears. "I wish you'd let me explain."

"I think you already did," he said.

He was way on the other side of the room. It felt so unfair that Matthew could walk away from her while she was stuck in bed, weak and half dressed.

"You're crazy, do you know that?" Matthew continued, pacing. "What you did is psychotic."

"Why is it psychotic if I did it, and brilliant if Alpha did it?" wailed Frankie. "That's so unfair. It's a double standard."

"He's getting expelled! You lied to me!" Matthew grabbed a small metal bowl from the nurse's desk and threw it against the wall. It hit the floor with a clatter.

"Don't throw things!" Frankie shouted. "You can't throw things."

"You're making me want to throw things!" cried Matthew.

"Well, stop!" She said it as strongly as she could.

Matthew paced some more, but he didn't throw anything else.

Neither of them spoke.

"I'm turning you in," Matthew finally said. "I'm going to Richmond's office right now."

He went through the door and slammed it behind him.

"Don't shut that door on me!" cried Frankie. "Come back!" She swung her legs off the infirmary cot and stumbled to the door in the cotton gown the nurse had given her.

She would stop him.

She would explain. Make him see how he'd misjudged her.

But by the time she opened the door, Matthew was already out of the building.

The Letter, Again

Ms. Jensson, the Cities teacher, had kept a photocopy of Frankie's paper on the activities of the Suicide Club and the Cacophony Society. When Richmond asked the faculty and students to come forward if they had any evidence that shed light on recent events, she turned it in. It contained numerous elements that could be identified as the seeds for the projects of the Loyal Order, and Ms. Jensson (who was eager to disassociate herself from the perpetrator in order to keep her new job) helpfully made notes for the headmaster so he wouldn't miss any of the connections.

The day after Matthew reported her, Richmond called Frankie to his office and requested a letter of confession. In response, she wrote the missive you no doubt remember from the start of this chronicle:

I, Frankie Landau-Banks, hereby confess that I was the sole mastermind behind the mal-doings of Loyal Order of the Basset Hounds. I take full responsibility for the disruptions caused by the Order—including the Library Lady, the Doggies in the Window, the Night of a Thousand Dogs, the Canned Beet Rebellion, and the abduction of the Guppy.

That is, I wrote the directives telling everyone what to do.

I. And I alone.

No matter what Porter Welsch told you in his statement . . .

Examination week began that same day, and Frankie was grateful. The semester's classes were over and the usual rhythms—meals, sports practice, dorm check-in times—were all suspended in favor of a test schedule.

Frankie, her arm bandaged and a prescription for antibiotics in her pocket, dropped the letter in Richmond's office and went up to the widow's walk to call Zada. She explained everything.

"Senior is going to lose his mind," Zada said after she'd listened.

"I know."

"Why did you want to be a member of his dumb old club anyway?"

"I don't know."

"I doubt he'll be mad that you wanted to be a member," said Zada. "I mean, I think it's like his dream that you follow in his footsteps. But he'll be furious you got the whole thing exposed and lost the *Disreputable History*. He'll think you showed disrespect to his sacred institution and compromised the secrecy of the club."

"Do you think he'll pull me out of school—if I'm not expelled?" asked Frankie. "Like, he'll refuse to pay for it anymore?"

"Maybe. But do you want to go to Alabaster anyway?"

Frankie did—and she didn't. She wanted the good education. She wanted the power that being an Alabaster alum would give her. She wanted the doors to open that Alabaster could open for her.

She was an ambitious person.

But she also hated the boarding school panopticon, the patriarchal establishment, the insular, overprivileged life. And she hated the thought of another half year in company with Matthew and Alpha, after what had happened. Part of her wished Richmond *would* expel her, the way he had been planning to expel

Alpha; or that Senior would refuse to pay, and the choice would be made for her.

"You can sic Ruth on him if he tries to pull you out," continued Zada, when Frankie didn't answer. "If she starts in on him, he'll keep you in school. He can't say no to her whenever it comes down to it."

"I know," said Frankie.

"Bunny, do you need to be on medication?" Zada asked suddenly.

"What?"

"I mean, should you maybe go have a chat with a counselor? It sounds like you're kind of—like you got obsessed."

"I think it's the institution," said Frankie.

"I'm not saying an institution, I'm just saying a counselor."

"No, it's the institution that's wrong with me," said Frankie.

"Alabaster?"

"I was trying to master it."

"Bunny, go talk to the counselor for one hour. I'll help you deal with Senior."

"I have a geometry test," Frankie told Zada. "I have to go now."

Outside Founder's House, Frankie ran into Porter. He had been waiting for her. "Let me walk you to geometry," he said, stepping onto the quad. "Are you ready for the test?"

Frankie shook her head. "I've been in the infirmary. I haven't studied that much."

The last time they had spoken, she'd been screaming at him in the Front Porch, but Porter acted as if nothing could be further from his mind. "I didn't know it was you," he said as they walked. "When I turned in those e-mails, I didn't know it was you."

"Oh."

"I thought it was Alpha. I mean, I know we've had our differences, and I was a jerk last year, but I wouldn't turn you in to Richmond like that. I had no idea. I would feel so bad if you got expelled because of what I did."

He still had an impulse to protect her—he who'd done her more damage than anyone. "Why did you turn them in at all?" Frankie asked. "Weren't you a member of the Loyal Order?"

Porter shook his head. "Not really," he said.

"How do you mean?"

"I was a spy." He said it with a glimmer of pride. "Last March, when Richmond let Alpha back in to Alabaster for senior year—he knew he was letting in a troublemaker. Alpha had broken all kinds of rules his first two years; he got caught with alcohol. And cigarettes. He snuck off campus. You know."

"Yeah, I know."

"Anyway," said Porter. "Richmond wanted to give Alpha a chance to graduate from Alabaster, but also wanted someone in the student body who could keep track of what Alpha was up to, because Alpha potentially wielded a lot of control over the senior boys."

Frankie looked at her feet, stepping in the muddy, packed snow of the unsanctioned path across the quad. "Why would you do something like that?"

"Richmond knew I was failing bio."

"You were?" Frankie hadn't known.

"I had blown off the homework at the start of the term and couldn't catch up. Puffert was threatening to make me repeat the class, but Richmond called me in and told me he could make the problem go away if I would do something for him. He knew I was friendly with Callum and Tristan from lacrosse, and asked if I would, you know, join the pack. And report back if anything major was brewing."

"Richmond knew about the Bassets?"

"No. The guy was clueless until all those dogs started popping up this year. He just told me to see if I could get in with those guys and keep an eye out. I knew that meant becoming a Basset, but that if I made the right moves it wouldn't be too hard."

"Why not?"

"My dad was a member, and my older brother, too.

325

Whole thing. I'm a legacy. So I was fairly certain I'd get the tap, if I only got those guys to like me."

"Didn't you think how upset your family would be when you betrayed the Order?"

Porter laughed bitterly. "Yeah, I thought about that."

"So how could you do it?"

"The last thing I want is to be like my dad, Frankie." Porter shook his head. "Or my brother. You should remember that. I hate everything they stand for."

"So you told Richmond yes."

Porter shrugged. "Yeah. I mean, I thought it over carefully. I'm not saying it was easy. But Richmond was rescuing me from repeating bio, I got to say F.U. to my dad, and in addition, it was a chance to knock Tesorieri off his perch."

"Uh-huh."

"I got new clothes, I joked around in the locker room, I showed up at parties even when I wasn't invited, until eventually—I was invited. It wasn't hard, really."

"What's your grudge with Alpha?" Frankie asked him.

"He went out with my sister Jeannie when they were sophomores. Didn't you know that?"

No, she didn't.

"He broke her heart. Completely stopped talking

326

to her one day. No notice, no formal breakup. She ended up sinking into a huge depression and spent all of the next summer locked in her bedroom, drinking and listening to The Smiths. Ruined."

"Oh."

"Yeah, my parents had to send her to a shrink." Porter took off his scarf and folded it neatly as he walked. "So I never liked the guy," he went on. "And then once I was in the Order, he was so full of himself. Sure, I had to admire his ideas—well, they were your ideas—but I hated the way he acted like he owned us. Leader of the pack. It just grated on me."

"What about Callum and Tristan? You didn't care about betraying them?"

"They're good to play lacrosse with. But they're—they're very clubby. Very old school. I'm a geek, Frankie. They're not like my real friends."

"Matthew made you apologize to me, didn't he?" Frankie guessed.

"I would have anyway."

"And he made you give him a printout."

"Well, yeah. He did. You knew about that?"

Frankie nodded. "I found it."

"He's not everything he seems, Frankie. I tried to warn you away from him at the Front Porch, but I couldn't say anything else because he got seriously mad that I asked you to come to lunch with me, and then even madder when he heard we'd been arguing."

"Really?"

"Yeah, for weeks I was getting these notes from Matthew every couple days, questioning my loyalty and telling me I'd better adhere to the code of the Bassets or lose my place. So there was no way I could report to Richmond or do anything but exactly what Alpha was telling me to do in the e-mails—or the Bassets would kick me out and the whole spy project would be for nothing."

"Only it wasn't Alpha writing the e-mails."

"No." He looked at her and pulled his winter cap down farther over his ears.

They were standing in front of the mathematics building now. Students were filing in for the eleven a.m. exam. "Anyway," said Porter. "I wanted to say that I didn't know those e-mails I turned in would implicate you. I'm sorry for all the trouble it's causing."

"What's the difference?" Frankie asked him.

"How do you mean?"

"What's the difference between me and Alpha? Why would you turn him in, and not me, if your mission was to turn in the person responsible?"

Porter frowned, thinking. "I have some kind of loyalty to you, I guess. Because we used to go out. I think you always have some kind of leftover loyalty to a person you went out with."

"And you don't have any loyalty to Tristan? Or Callum?"

He shrugged. "I was never really there, you know? I was just pretending to be there."

Neither of them knew what to say for a minute. Frankie scuffed her boot in the snow.

"Why did you do all that, Frankie?" asked Porter. "I mean, it was brilliant, what you did, what you made us do—but why would you bother? That's what I can't figure out."

Frankie sighed. "Have you ever heard of the panopticon?" she asked him.

Porter shook his head.

"Have you ever been in love?"

He shook his head again.

"Then I can't explain it," Frankie said.

They went inside and took the geometry test.

Some More E-mail

○

*I*N SOME WAYS, we can see Frankie Landau-Banks as a neglected positive. A buried word.

A word inside another word that's getting all the attention.

A mind inside a body that's getting all the attention.

Frankie's mind is a word overlooked, but when uncovered—through invention, imagination, or recollection—it wields a power that is comical, surprising, and memorable.

Now, not only is it true that a student with significant family wealth is less likely to be kicked out of a fancy boarding school than is a scholarship student, it is also true that a sweet-looking girl with no prior record of misbehavior gets a more lenient sentence (even with a full, written confession) than would a senior boy with a history of visits to the headmaster's office.

Headmaster Richmond and the committee on discipline agreed to keep both Alpha and Frankie at Alabaster on probation. They let her know two days before the end of winter exams.

And Frankie found that she wanted to stay.

Or rather, she chose to stay, even though she also found it terrifying. In the long run, staying was more likely to get her where she wanted to go. Wherever that was. Wherever that is. Because the education, and the connections, and the Alabaster reputation were worth the trouble—even though Matthew and his friends were forever lost to her.

Winter break. Hannukah. Ruth, the vile pack of boys, Zada home with a suitcase full of hippie clothes and feminist literature. I will not tire you with details except to say that Frankie's position at family gatherings was slightly different.

She had surprised everyone.

They were not sure quite where she fit in anymore. If she was not Bunny Rabbit, as it was finally clear she was not—who was she? Senior, down for a visit, could not look her in the eye. Ruth squeezed her shoulders frequently but rarely engaged in conversation. Uncle Paul and Uncle Ben refrained from their usual questions about boys and school, settling instead for offering to play a game of Monopoly when they came over for a holiday meal.

Frankie beat them both easily.

December 22nd, after a big family dinner of latkes and applesauce, complete with Paulie Junior throwing a potted plant out a second-floor window and paying the smallest of the vile cousins to run all the way around the block with no shirt on, Frankie closed herself in her room and opened her laptop. At the top of the screen was her Gmail icon. Messages: 1.

She hadn't had mail at thealphadog since Matthew had turned her in.

From: Alessandro Tesorieri [at114@alabasterpreparatory.edu]
To: thealphadog@gmail.com
Subject: A compliment, believe it or not

I've thought about writing you, a lot—but then I didn't.
I don't think you deserve it, seriously.

But then I keep remembering the work.

The plotting, and the access to the buildings, and the letters and the e-mails.

Even the shopping.

Getting all those dogs to do your bidding.

I remember that you made Matthew and everyone—the whole school, even—think I was a genius.

That I was the guy I'd like to be. The guy I'm not, really. The guy who has the cockfights and the drag races.

The amount of time it must have taken you to do all that is phenomenal.

Psychopathic, probably.

I took credit for everything, yes. Because it was all freaking brilliant, and I'm a brilliant guy sometimes, but I don't always act on it.

I don't really act on it.

I'm gonna be sorry I sent this. It's late at night and I've been drinking. My mom is freaking crazy. She wants to move us to California so she can try and be on television.
The woman is 43.

It's not like I want to be friends with you now, Frankie. Don't even talk to me, I seriously can't deal with you.

I'm just writing to say I underestimated you.
I significantly underestimated you.
I don't actually think it is possible to *over*estimate you.
Although you are not a nice person.

Alpha

Frankie's heart jumped at the letter. Victorious and hopeful.

She had impressed Alpha.

Won his admiration.

Was this what she'd really been trying to do all along?

For a brief moment she thought about writing back. Despite what he'd said, despite everything that had happened, maybe they could be friends. Maybe even something more. They were alike, he and she, in so many ways. And now he had finally recognized himself in her, or herself in him.

Had he not?

But she wanted something more than Alpha. She did. Something much more.

So she did not reply, but played the strategist. She retained more power by withholding an answer.

AFTER THE FALL, SPRING

◉

WHEN FRANKIE RETURNED to Alabaster at the start of the winter term, she was something of a celebrity. Star and Claudia shunned her for getting Alpha and his pack in trouble, as did Elizabeth and numerous other seniors, while Trish stood by her staunchly. The people in the Debate Club and the rest of the Geek Club Conglomerate elevated her to legendary status and asked her to sit at their tables in the caf. Members of student government were surprisingly interested in discussing strategies for social change, and the AVT guys got inspired and began regularly sneaking into the new theater at midnight (since they had keys) and screening films for their friends.

Frankie appreciated both the accolades and the

rejections equally, because both meant she'd had an impact. She wasn't a person who needed to be liked so much as she was a person who liked to be notorious.

As a condition of her return to Alabaster, Ruth and Zada insisted Frankie begin counseling. She sat through weekly sessions with the school mental health professional in order to explore her "aggression" and to work on channeling her impulses into more socially appropriate activities. The counselor suggested competitive team sports as a positive outlet, and pushed Frankie to join the girls' field hockey team.

That was not a productive solution.

It was the girls' team.

Boys didn't even play field hockey.

Boys thought nothing of field hockey.

Frankie was not interested in playing a sport that was rated as nothing by the more powerful half of the population.

The counselor also suggested meditation. Finding a bit of time each day to focus on deep breathing and the acceptance of life as it was presently occurring.

That was not a productive solution either.

Frankie did not accept life as it was presently occurring. It was a fundamental element of her character. Life as it was presently occurring was not acceptable to her. Were she to mellow out—would she not become obedient? Would she not stay on the path that stretched ahead of her, nicely bricked?

She did not get much out of therapy.

Frankie Landau-Banks is an off-roader.

She might, in fact, go crazy, as has happened to a lot of people who break rules. Not the people who play at rebellion but really only solidify their already dominant positions in society—as did Matthew and most of the other Bassets—but those who take some larger action that disrupts the social order. Who try to push through the doors that are usually closed to them. They do sometimes go crazy, these people, because the world is telling them not to want the things they want. It can seem saner to give up—but then one goes insane from giving up.

On the brighter side, Frankie has life easier than a lot of people with similar drives, similar minds, similar ambitions. She is nice-looking and will be well educated. Her family has a good amount of money, though not as much as some. Many doors will open to her easily, and it may be that she can open the ones she wants to without too much pain or strife.

And so, another possibility—the possibility I hold out for—is that Frankie Landau-Banks will open the doors she is trying to get through.

And she will grow up to change the world.

As we leave her, Frankie is finishing her sophomore

year. From the outside, it appears she's doing well. Behaving as everyone wants her to behave. But the burn on her arm left a wicked scar from elbow to wrist, and she wears long sleeves even in hot weather to keep the mangled skin away from prying eyes.

She's still taking modern dance, still debating, still rooming with Trish, who has settled on viewing all Frankie's behavior during the ignominious fall as "stress from a bad relationship."

Frankie is grateful to have such a loyal friend, but it does not escape her notice that Trish's lack of understanding is a condition of that loyalty. Were Trish to fully comprehend the way Frankie thinks, the subjects she ponders all the time when she appears to be quietly doing her homework—Frankie's anger and hunger—she would pull away. To Trish, Frankie is still the ordinary girl with gerbils at home in a Habitrail, only now more melancholy and in need of cheering up, due to the second bad boyfriend in a row.

There's Frankie now, sitting with laptop on a bench in front of the library in the warm spring air. It's a Saturday. Most of the students have taken one of the Alabaster shuttles to town, and the campus is largely empty. Trish is playing golf with Artie.

Matthew, Dean, and Callum burst out of Hazelton and hurtle down the steps, then stand around talking about ten feet from Frankie, before heading in their separate directions.

They don't say hello.

They don't even appear to see her.

"I could care less about crew this year," Callum is saying.

"Couldn't care less!" Matthew says, poking him. "If you could care less, that means you care a fairly decent amount. It's *couldn't* care less."

"Dog, I know that. You told me before. I just don't care."

Matthew laughs. "But you know it's like nails on the chalkboard of my brain. Can't you say it right, just for me?"

"Dog," jokes Callum. "I'm going to sneak into that brain of yours in the middle of the night and massacre your inner copy editor. No wonder you don't have a girlfriend."

"You did it again!" cries Matthew, giggling and banging his shoulder against Callum's.

"What?'

"You can't massacre it! *Massacre* refers to the slaughter of many people," explains Matthew. "You'd have to murder it. Or assassinate it. Because it's only one."

Callum smiles. "Dog, it is obvious to everyone that you have many, many copy editors in there."

"Touché."

Dean interjects. "You guys want to play golf tonight?"

"Absolutely," Matthew says. "I'll get the word out." A pause. "Me and my copy editors."

Frankie almost laughs out loud, but she knows she is not supposed to be listening.

And of course no one plays golf at night, not without infrared goggles.

They are having a party.

Suddenly, Frankie's protective armor is gone and she is not angry at anyone about anything anymore. Looking at Matthew, she sees nothing but a beautiful boy who used to think she was adorable. A boy who loves words, who makes her laugh. She sees his knowing smile, big shoulders, and the sun-kissed freckles across his nose. His Superman T-shirt still lives in the bottom of Frankie's drawer, and all she sees is a boy whose world is lit up with adventure and confidence and humor and friendship. It was a world she used to be—almost was—welcome in.

Frankie wants to go to the party on the golf course. She is sorry for everything. She wishes she had never infiltrated the Bassets. She wishes she were a different kind of girl. Someone simple, sweet, and unambitious.

Maybe she could be that girl. Maybe there is a chance.

"Matthew," Frankie calls as he heads down the stairs away from her.

She can tell from the way his back stiffens that he has heard. But he doesn't answer.

"Matthew!" she calls again. "Hey, listen!"

He turns.

Does he still think she is pretty?

Does he remember how it felt when they kissed in his narrow dorm-room bed? When they held hands in the dark?

Matthew is gallant. He has been brought up well. Noblesse oblige. Although he has not looked Frankie in the eye since he left the infirmary that day, he does so now that she's spoken to him. A spasm of disgust crosses his face for just a moment before he forces it away. "Yes?"

"I have this T-shirt I should give back to you," Frankie tells him.

Will he come get the shirt? Will he come now, to her room, and they will be alone together, and everything bad will just wash away?

"I don't remember," he says, sounding nonchalant.

But of course he remembers. Frankie knows this game.

"Superman," she says. "The Superman T-shirt."

"Oh, I forgot." He is laughing slightly. Fake. "Keep it," he says. "I never take back my gifts."

Matthew would rather let her keep the shirt than interact with Frankie for another second. He hates her that much.

He turns away, and the dogs follow.

Frankie chokes back tears. She doesn't want the shirt anyway.

As the Bassets head across the lawn, Frankie reminds herself why she doesn't want Matthew. Doesn't want him anyway.

It is better to be alone, she figures, than to be with someone who can't see who you are. It is better to lead than to follow. It is better to speak up than stay silent. It is better to open doors than to shut them on people.

She will not be simple and sweet. She will not be what people tell her she should be. That Bunny Rabbit is dead.

She watches the boys as they peel off in different directions and disappear around corners and into the buildings of Alabaster.

She doesn't feel like crying anymore.

*A few notes on the text,
plus grateful acknowledgments*

I AM INDEBTED to a number of books for my ideas about boarding school, boys clubs, pranks, interventionist art, urban exploration, and so on. In particular, I made use of: *Fugitives and Refugees: A Walk in Portland, Oregon* by Chuck Palahnuik; *The Interventionists: Users' Manual for the Creative Disruption of Everyday Life* edited by Nato Thompson and Gregory Sholette; *Preparing for Power: America's Elite Boarding Schools* by Peter W. Cookson Jr. and Caroline Hodges Persell; *If at All Possible, Involve a Cow: The Book of College Pranks* by Neil Steinberg; *Prank University: The Ultimate Guide to College's Greatest Tradition* by John Austin; *The Code of the Woosters* and the Drones Club stories by P. G. Wodehouse; *Brideshead Revisited* by Evelyn Waugh; and *The Suicide Club*, by Robert Louis Stevenson.

I did research at Web sites such as santarchy.com,

museumofhoaxes.com, actionsquad.org, la.cacophony.org, bridesofmarch.org, and numerous others devoted to urban exploration or college pranks.

The material in Frankie's Suicide Club/Cacophony Society paper is factual, as is the material on the panopticon, the theoretical interpretation of which comes very loosely from *Discipline and Punish: The Birth of the Prison* by Michel Foucault. The theft of the Guppy is based on the 1933 theft of the Sacred Cod of Massachusetts, which was stolen by students from Harvard. It is one of the most famous college pranks of all time. All errors regarding these crazy subjects are my own.

The information about secret societies is completely imaginary—and probably false.

The basset hound of vegetables was inspired by my friend Paul Zelinsky, who once made a Rapunzel out of cheese.

Thank you to Donna Bray for her great leniency and editorial acumen. And for her faith that I would write something decent from a proposal that was nothing more than two paragraphs of silliness. Everyone at Hyperion has been wonderfully supportive and creative, in particular Emily Schultz, Elizabeth Clark, Jennifer Zatorski, Scottie Bowditch, and Angus Killick. My agent, Elizabeth Kaplan, is indispensable. I am so grateful for her help.

Thank you to Ben Fine for his boarding school stories, and to my friends from college who threw late-night parties on the Vassar golf course. My husband let me steal some of his jokes and read an early draft.

Justine Larbalestier, Maryrose Wood, Lauren Myracle, and Sarah Mlynowski kibbitzed on my author picture so much it felt like we were having a pajama party, and then they made me go back and have a new one taken wearing makeup—thank you, all. Heather Weston (heatherweston.com) took endless photos and charged me only an eighth of what they are worth.

Sarah Mlynowski read a draft when this book was in terrible, half-finished form and helped me immensely. Much appreciation also to the members of my YA Novelists newsgroup for weighing in on the title and in general for their support. Thank you to my writing companions, Scott Westerfeld, Maureen Johnson, and John Green, for keeping me from being lonely during revisions and for answering tedious questions such as "What is the little show in Ms. Pac-Man called, you know, the thing that happens after you've completed two thingees?" (intermission between levels) or "What is that band you listen to when you're really depressed?" (The Smiths)—whenever I asked.